also by
~ஓ~Phillip Hardy~ஓ~

The James Harding Novels
Lone Oak
Fool's Gold

Phillip Hardy

VENGEANCE
IS MINE

A James Harding Novel

GELAN
Livonia, Michigan

VENGEANCE IS MINE
Copyright © 2017 Phillip Hardy

Published by Gelan
an imprint of BHC Press

Library of Congress Control Number:
2017935175

ISBN: 978-1-946006-82-0

www.bhcpress.com

To my family
who encouraged me through
some of the toughest times of my life.
I love you all.

VENGEANCE

IS MINE

Prologue

tepping up to the batwings, Jim looked inside. He searched the room for any other members of the gang that might be present and let his eyes adjust to the dim interior before entering. Seevers and Gates seemed to be the only two outlaws present. Pushing through the doors, Jim glanced around one more time before speaking.

"Seevers, Gates, drink up and enjoy. It's your last one this side of Hell. You butchered my parents and sister and put the whip and hot coals to me. Today you pay."

The two spun around to see who the speaker might be. Seevers recovered first and went for his gun. The space between the combatants cleared instantly as Jim's rifle began to spout flame and lead. The first bullet shattered Seevers's wrist, and the second one smashed Gates's remaining elbow. The next few seconds were filled with the sound of gunfire as Jim emptied his rifle into two men who were part of the group that had taught him to hate. The two knew terror as they were shot full of holes by someone they thought they had killed two years before. They knew terror and then death, and then the flames of Hell welcomed them to their final destiny.

One

The aspens on the hills were changing to their brilliant autumn golds while the maples and oaks added their vibrant reds to the symphony of September colors. The nearby Rockies already had their first dash of termination dust and would soon have their cold blanket of winter snow.

Dan Harding took it all in and was content. No, he was more than content, he was happy. This was his home, the Lazy H, a ranch that he had worked and saved for years to start, and now it was beginning to flourish. The cattle would be ready for market soon, and he had even found a rich vein of gold near one of the streams that crisscrossed his range.

As a former Montana Ranger, he knew better than to bring it out in large quantities, but there was no way to hide how rich the vein was because of the quality of ore that he brought in. He kept the location a secret against the possibility of claim jumpers. At forty-five, Dan was full of life and vitality. His years had been spent doing the things that made a man a man. He had trapped the nearby mountain streams and fought the Blackfoot, Crow, and Cheyenne, when he had to. He traded with them when he could and found them to be far better friends than enemies.

Ruthie, his bride of almost twenty years, joined him near the corral. The two stood side-by-side enjoying the crisp autumn air and each other's company. "Well, Ruthie, my beautiful bride, I think we're finally home to stay. No more chasing owl-hoots or escorting prisoners to where they don't want to be."

Ruthie smiled up at him in response. Her face still shined with as much love and adoration as it did on their wedding day. "That sure sounds wonderful to me. As long as it's with you, I'm satisfied."

They stood for a few more minutes with her head against his chest and his arm around her shoulders before starting off to do their morning chores. Their two teenage children, James, who his mother called Jimmy, and Rachael, had already started their daily to-dos and would be ready for breakfast soon. Rachael, who at sixteen was becoming a woman, would soon have breakfast on the table. Ruthie needed to get the milking done before then.

Seventeen-year-old Jimmy would be off checking the reservoir to make sure that no animals had fallen into it or become mired in the muddy areas surrounding the manmade lake. Dan had had to remind him to take his rifle in case of an emergency. One never knew when they might need the means to defend themselves in the Montana wilderness. He could shoot as well as any man in the area, handling a rifle or hand-gun as if they were an extension of himself. He would come running when the chow call came. All was as it should be.

As Dan began to fork hay to the horses in the corral, several riders began a rapid approach to the ranch. In the lead was Jacobs. He was the one hand that had worked for the Hard-ings. Dan had caught him stealing and had fired him instantly.

The rest were hard men, tough men who were drawn in by the lure of gold.

Jacobs knew about the gold but not where it came from. He figured that with this group backing him he could force Dan to talk. In his calculating he forgot that this was the man who had single-handedly brought in Black Jack Thompson and two other members of his gang alive. That was after making them bury the rest of the gang that died in the preceding shootout. That kind of man doesn't buffalo easily.

Storming into the yard with thirteen men at his back, Jacobs started to make his demands. He failed to notice the twin six-guns riding on Dan's hips.

"All right, Harding," he shouted as the rest of his gang fought their mounts to a halt. "We want the gold you been digging out! Where is it?"

"Jacobs, I fired you once for stealing. I gave you a break and didn't run you in. Now I'm going to give you another one and some advice. Get off my place and stay off. Try an honest day's work for an honest day's pay. That's your break and advice. Now it's your choice," was Dan's calm reply. He knew that if things blew up he was a dead man, but he didn't plan to go quietly, nor alone.

"C'mon, Jacobs. You promised us gold, now where is it?" snarled one of the hardcases.

"He'll talk," replied Jacobs. "He's got family to think about."

Just then Ruthie stepped from the barn with a milk pail in her hand. Seeing an obvious threat to her man, she dropped the pail and rushed forward to his aid. One of the men in the crowd was startled and fired.

Thrown backward by the impact, Ruthie landed on her back. Her sightless eyes stared into the blue autumn sky as blood soaked the front of her dress. Ruthie who had loved him when he was yet wild; Ruthie who had borne his two children and taught him the joys of family; his one and only love and the one who had tamed him lay dead on the ground.

Dan snapped. Deep within him the wildness that had been tamed by Ruthie sprang to the surface. Twin six-guns leaped from their holsters, and in less than a second, the man who had fired the first shot was blown from his saddle with two forty-five caliber holes in his chest less than a hand's breadth apart. The rearing of Jacobs's horse saved his life as the animal took the bullet intended for him between the eyes. The man who reminded Jacobs that they had come for gold fell to the ground with a "third eye" in his forehead. Then the return fire began.

Dan's left leg was knocked from under him, but he felt no pain. He only felt the burning desire to destroy those who had brought death to his home. His left hand Colt slipped from numb fingers as a heavy slug smashed his shoulder. The firer would never get the chance to correct his aim. Dan's next shot punched his final ticket. Two more shots from Dan shattered one criminal's arm and burrowed a hole through the thigh of another.

He had made his way to his beloved Ruthie where he absorbed the impact of several more heavy slugs before crumpling to the ground. He was by her side, inseparable in death just as they had been in life.

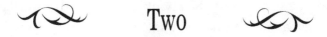

Two

Jimmy saw the dust from the approaching riders but paid little attention. Visitors were rare but not unheard of, and he had work to do before breakfast. Whoever it was would still be there when he returned. It would be nice to talk to someone other than his folks or Rachael. He smiled as he returned to his chore. Then the gunfire started. His father never allowed gunfire in the ranch yard unless it was an emergency. Putting spurs to the chestnut gelding he was riding, he raced recklessly toward his family.

As he sprinted his horse into the ranch yard, Jimmy took in the carnage and charged forward. He leaped from the back of his thundering mount and swept his rifle to his shoulder. The rifle barked, and the man with a hole in his leg would now need an undertaker rather than a doctor. A shot from one of the outlaws struck him a glancing blow to the head rendering him unconscious, but not before his rifle sent its message of revenge through the heart of another attacker.

In a matter of minutes the number of attackers had been reduced by a third, and one of those still alive would probably lose his right arm. There had been no gold found, and all of them would now be wanted men. They would be wanted for the murder of a Montana Ranger and even worse, his wife. It didn't matter that the man who had fired the fatal shot was himself dead. Western men would hold them all responsible for her death.

A commotion from the house followed by a young woman's screams drew the attention of all of the attackers. A burly, unshaven man had Rachael by the arm and was dragging her from the house.

"Lookie here what I caught," the bearded ruffian said with a wicked grin. His foul breath rolled out from between the gaps in his broken and rotted teeth. "If 'n we can't find no gold, I'm gonna get something to make the trip worthwhile."

Jacobs stepped in. "I've got a better idea, Daily." He smiled. It wasn't for decency that he interrupted the brute but greed. A cruel smile played on his lips.

"Now listen here, little missy. You tell us where your pa's gold strike is and we'll let you loose. If not, I'll just give you back to Daily and the rest of them. You'll wish you were dead before they're done with you. Tell me where it is. It's your only hope."

"You're a beast," Rachael fumed. She wrenched her right hand free and struck Jacobs across the face. "I don't know where it is, and if I did, I wouldn't tell the likes of you." Her youth gave her a bravado that she really did not feel. What she really wanted to do was cry, but she wouldn't give them the satisfaction. Her parents had instilled that much iron into her while still trying to make her a lady.

A slight welt was rising on Jacobs's cheek, and he heard the snickers of the others. "This is your last chance," he snarled. "Tell me where it is or back to Daily you go."

Fear crept into Rachael's eyes, but she stood defiant.

"Fine," Jacobs growled. "Back to Daily you go! Daily, boys, here's a gift." He shoved her roughly back to her original captor. Hurling her to the ground, Daily pounced on her like the animal that he was, but he didn't anticipate Rachael's courage nor resourcefulness. As he struggled to pin her down, Rachael pulled one of Daily's pistols and shot him in the belly. He reared back in surprise and pain. Then she shot him again under his chin. The bullet came to rest inside the back of his skull and his body slumped forward on top of her.

Rachael squirmed from under her attacker's body with the pistol in hand ready to defend her home. As she rose to her feet, she faced one of the outlaws ready to continue the fight. Another one raced his horse from behind her and trampled her underfoot as she raised the pistol to fire at the nearest of her home's attackers.

Jimmy recovered consciousness just enough to see his sister trampled by an outlaw on a dappled gray gelding with four white stockings. He tried to cry out, but all he could manage was a low, croaking groan. It was enough to draw the attention of the killers though. As he struggled to make sense of the scene before him, two of the attackers rushed forward to tackle him before he recovered his wits enough to put up resistance.

Darkness enveloped him once again. He wasn't aware of being hauled to the middle of the yard and tied to the hitching rail. He was unaware of his shirt being torn from his back exposing his bare skin to the punishment to come. He was unaware of anything until the icy water shocked him back to consciousness. With consciousness came the memory of what he had seen. As he struggled to find the means to continue the fight, he discovered his bonds.

"No sense struggling, Jimmy boy," came a voice he knew he should recognize. Turning toward the voice and pushing the fog from his brain, James recognized Jacobs with sudden clarity.

"Jacobs, you lowlife. Pa fired you for stealing, and you dare to show your face back on our spread. Get off and stay off!" Anger and another emotion he had never felt before, hatred, mixed together in young James Harding's soul.

That's when the pain started. The first lash of the black-snake whip bit deep into his flesh. After his first instinctive cry of pain, James clamped his teeth together and bore the beating in silence. His father had taught him to bear up under pain by concentrating on verses from the Bible. James concentrated on a very small part of one verse leaving out much of the verse including, "Saith the Lord." He ran over and over in his mind the portion of Romans 12:19 that said, "Vengeance is mine, I will repay," as he memorized names and faces.

"It can stop any time, Jimmy boy," taunted Jacobs. "All you have to do is tell us where the gold is."

Some of the men unfamiliar with the use of the whip used their coiled ropes to inflict their own sadistic torture. At last James passed out again. When his senses returned, it was to find himself tied spread eagle in the ranch yard. A small fire was burning nearby.

"Wakey wakey, Jimmy boy," purred Jacobs. He seemed to derive a great deal of pleasure from the pain inflicted on the son of the man who had fired him.

As James took in the scene around him, he caught bits and pieces of the conversation going on. "I thought we'd killed him already but there he is."

"His old man was tougher than nails. It must run in the family." One comment held his attention and gave him an idea of why they had built a fire. "You put those coals to him and he'll talk. Nobody can take that."

"Tell me where the gold is and the pain will stop." It was Jacobs again. "That's all we want. We didn't want this to happen, but your folks were unreasonable. You don't have to go through this."

"Come closer," whispered James. "I've got something to tell you. It's for your ears only."

"Ha! You see, I knew he'd come around," Jacobs bellowed triumphantly.

He knelt down next to James and leaned closer to him. Suddenly James lunged as far as his bonds would permit and head butted the outlaw before spitting in his face. "I've seen pigs that were better people than you, Jacobs. I will see all of you hang for this if I don't kill you myself!"

He steeled himself against what was to come but still cried out when the hot coals began to burn into his flesh.

"Somebody's coming!" shouted one of the lookouts. Sure enough, there was dust in the distance raised by a large party of horsemen.

"Let's get out of here!" came the cry, and panic set in. All of the thieves ran for their mounts leaving young James still tied with the hot coals searing into his chest. Turning, one of the outlaws fired some parting shots in James's direction. The first one struck the cords holding his left hand and he twisted violently throwing the coals from his chest. Two more of the shots struck James, but because he had twisted so violently, they missed the vital organs they were intended to hit. Even so, it would take a miracle and much time for him to heal.

Three

The dust that had been seen by the outlaws was raised by a Cheyenne hunting party. Upon hearing the shots from the ranch of someone who let them pass through unmolested and occasionally let them have a beef or two raised the party's curiosity. The retreating dust cloud added to it.

Taking two scouts, including his only son, with him, the leader of the party rode warily toward the ranch. Leaving their ponies hidden in one of the ravines near the ranch house, the scouting party advanced silently on foot.

The attackers had fled leaving their own dead among the bodies of their victims. The sign was easy to read. Six of their number were dead, and the sign pointed to another being seriously wounded. They had also lost a horse and failed to carry away anything noticeable.

As the three Cheyenne spread out to search for anything useful among what they thought were ten dead white eyes, the older of the two scouts found the empty right hand Colt of Dan Harding. He excitedly showed it to the others in his group and carefully tucked away his new treasure. He would use it in many battles, he told himself as he stripped the ammunition from Dan's gun belt.

After collecting the weapons of the dead attackers, curiosity led the braves to examine what they were sure was James's body. Not sure why James was found the way he was, they began to talk among themselves. Dan had taught his son and daughter how to speak Cheyenne, Blackfoot, Crow, and Sioux. He believed that they should be able to talk to the tribes from the area if need be.

As the voices invaded James's brain, he responded. "I'll tell you nothing!" he shouted in Cheyenne.

Startled, the three began talking excitedly. "How can he talk? He's dead."

The bloody mass of humanity that lay before them could not possibly be alive. Shock, the whip and rope lashing, the bullet holes, and the horrible burn on his chest was more than anyone could survive. Here he was, though, talking to them, and in Cheyenne!

The leader of the scouting party decided to bring the entire hunting party to the ranch. There was food, horses, and cattle that the Cheyenne could use, and these white eyes would no longer need them. Besides, he was curious to see if this son of a Montana Ranger would live or die. It didn't matter to him, but he was curious. If he lived through the night, they would take him along and nurse him back to health. If not, he wasn't Cheyenne anyway.

As the Indian camp was set up a short distance from the ranch yard, Two Bears, the band's leader, told the rest of the party what they had found. He ended the tale by telling of them finding James still alive and speaking to them in Cheyenne. "If he lives through the night," Two Bears said, "then he is chosen for a purpose and cannot die." The rest of the leaders nodded in agreement.

James was carried to the camp and watched through the night. Each time the medicine man thought James was about to breathe his last, James would speak through clenched teeth. Sometimes he would say a few words, sometimes a name or two. "Vengeance is mine, I will repay," was repeated in English, Cheyenne, Crow, Sioux, Blackfoot, or a combination of the languages.

As the last stars faded from the night sky and a gray haze filled the eastern horizon, James began to breathe more evenly and a more restful sleep finally found him.

FOR THREE DAYS the Cheyenne watched and waited while young James Harding fought for his life. After the first night the medicine man applied herbs and ointments to the many wounds covering his body. They warded off infections that would have surely killed him. Under the shaman's watchful care, James began to recover.

About noon the fourth day after the raid, James sat bolt upright brushing furiously at his chest as if the hot coals still sat upon it. Panic and confusion filled his eyes as his mind tried to comprehend the scene around him. He had been unconscious for four days, and what he saw now was not the scene that he had left four days earlier. Gone were the cruel faces of the bandits. In their place were the impassive faces of Cheyenne warriors along with the curious stares of their women and children.

Two Bears and the medicine man came closer and stared down on him.

"So, Can't Die still lives. What did I say that first night, Grey Cloud?" Two Bears asked. His normally impassive face formed what could be imagined was a smile as he thumped the medicine man soundly on the back.

"Only because of my great ability,"Grey Cloud replied smugly.

The two walked away. Grey Cloud ordered that Can't Die be fed. It had been several days since James had eaten, and his mother's favorite dairy cow tasted excellent in the thick stew that a young Indian maiden fed him.

James, now called Can't Die by the entire camp, recovered slowly. The physical wounds would heal, but his body would carry the scars for the rest of his life. His mind and soul would be tormented by the images of his family being murdered long after his body healed. Those wounds would take the longest to heal.

When Two Bears ordered the camp to pack up and move out, they took James with them. They also took horses, cattle, and anything else that they thought might be of use. James was in no shape to argue even if he wanted to. He did, however, convince Two Bears to give his family a proper burial.

"Leave the scum to rot, but please give my family the dignity they deserve. My father would have done the same for you."

"You speak the truth, Can't Die. We will honor your family," Two Bears replied. He had the bodies of the attackers dragged from the yard and ordered that the Hardings be buried properly.

Even though James was a white man, he spent the next two years living with his Cheyenne rescuers. During that time he learned how to track far beyond what his father had taught him. He learned the use of the bow and war club. He also learned trapping and hunting skills as well as silent movement, mounted combat, and more. Because of his ordeal, the Cheyenne readily accepted him as an honorary member of the tribe.

Now, almost nineteen, and fully recovered physically, it was time for James to return home or at least to his people. In his mind it was also time for his family's killers to face justice, or vengeance. They were both the same to him.

On the eve of his departure James saw Two Bears's oldest son, Standing Buffalo, practicing with a six-gun that looked very familiar. As he looked more closely at the weapon in the hand of someone who was a close friend, he realized that it was one of his father's.

"Standing Buffalo, where did you get that?" There was an unintentional challenge in James's voice as he asked the question.

"I found it," was the simple, honest reply.

"It is my father's. Give it to me!"

"I told you, I found it. It is mine!"

The pistol was a superb weapon and not something to be surrendered easily.

Two Bears appeared on the scene and silenced both young men. "Since both claim the pistol and neither will yield it, there is but one way to decide."

A circle of braves quickly formed and into the ring the pistol was tossed. The two friends, who were now combatants, were shoved roughly into the ring as well.

Warily the two circled one another looking for an advantage. They had wrestled before but never seriously. Both knew how dangerous their opponent could be.

As they came together, they both displayed great ability, strength, and agility. James's natural coordination was obvious, but Standing Buffalo was a noted wrestler in the camp. His quickness and agility made up for his smaller size. The match was very even until James switched tactics. The Cheyenne fought well, but they did not box. James had learned from his father who had learned from a master pugilist. Even so, Standing Buffalo withstood the punishing blows bravely and tried to battle back.

Standing Buffalo stumbled and James leaped on him intending to finish him off. As the young Cheyenne tried to rise, James locked an arm around his opponent's throat. Suddenly, the gravity of what he was about to do struck him. This was his friend and the son of the man who had saved his life. Wasn't that worth more than a pistol?

James flipped both combatants so that Standing Buffalo landed on top with James on his back under him. He threw both arms out wide and shouted, "I yield!" ending the contest.

As the two fighters came to their feet, James walked over to the pistol and picked it up. Turning, he carried it to Standing Buffalo. "My father would be honored to have his pistol carried by such a fine warrior. May you use it wisely in defense of your family. May your enemies know its sting and fear it. It is yours." He extended the weapon to his friend who graciously accepted it.

The next morning the whole camp turned out to see Can't Die off on his quest. Several of the women had made him moccasins, shirts, pants, or food for the journey. One of the warriors gave him a strong buffalo bow and a quiver of arrows. A repeating rifle and twenty bullets was a gift from Standing Buffalo.

Grey Cloud and Two Bears brought the final gift. Each presented him with three excellent horses for his vengeance quest. It seemed ironic that four of them were wearing his father's Lazy H brand and the other two had belonged to two of those who had slaughtered his family. Attached to the bridle of the lead horse was a leather pouch. While not a much bigger than a large marble bag, it was quite heavy.

"Your people place a high value on the yellow metal and its dust. Use what is there wisely," Two Bears grunted in farewell. James mounted and rode toward the nearest white settlement three days ride from the camp. He glanced back over his shoulder only once.

Four

He rode into town drawing the stares of many of the town's people. He knew that he would, dressed as he was. His white man's clothing had been replaced with a soft doeskin shirt with fancy beadwork across the front. A wide beaded belt wrapped around his lean waist carrying a razor sharp skinning knife in the sheath on his left hip. Instead of the breechclout and leggings that his Indian friends wore, he did wear pants made of well-tanned and softened leather. On his feet he wore moccasins made special for him by the daughter of Two Bears's brother. The chestnut gelding that he rode wore his father's Lazy H brand and a fine Winchester repeating rifle rode across the pommel of his saddle. Five excellent horses trailed behind him tied nose to tail.

Stopping at the assayer's office, James swung down from the saddle. Mounting the stairs to the office, he carried his rifle and the leather pouch that had been given to him by Two Bears. He remembered his father's dealings with his gold so had an idea of about how much he had and its value. That was good for him and bad for the assayer if he tried to cheat James. His father had instilled in him a distaste for thieves, and the events involving Jacobs and his gang had changed that from

27

disgust to a deep loathing for them. He considered a cheat in the same category.

The assayer looked up when James entered the office. He took in James's youth and Indian attire and smiled inwardly. "How can I help you, sir?" he began with a crooked smile.

When the gold-filled pouch was placed on the counter in front of him, his eyes gleamed greedily. "I've got some gold I want converted to cash. Can you help me out?"

Opening the pouch, the assayer poured the contents into a tray to be placed on the scale. After a quick examination of the dust and nuggets, he commented, "I can maybe go fifteen dollars an ounce. It's not that I can't use it, it's just that it will take some refining to get the impurities out. I may even lose money on it, but I'll take that chance…"

His voice trailed off as he noticed the muzzle of the Winchester move from pointing at the ceiling to pointing at his favorite watch chain right where it crossed his favorite belly-button. His eyes grew large and he licked his lips.

"My father raised me to be an honest man and to despise dishonesty. A bunch of murdering thieves killed him, my mother, and my sister. I detest thieves and liars. There's at least three pounds of pure gold in that pouch. It will take very little refining. My father was getting twenty dollars per ounce for his dust. I'll take that much for my estimated measure. I'm sure you'll still make a hefty profit and I'll be satisfied too. If not, I'll go elsewhere." James spoke with a quiet air of authority for one so young.

As the assayer looked up from the rifle muzzle to the young face, he started to protest. "Now see here, young man, you can't…" His voice stopped again as he looked into the icy blue eyes of the young man before him. There was no flinching in James, and his face betrayed no emotion.

"It's your choice, mister. If you think I'm wrong, I'll just take my business elsewhere."

The assayer knew that he would make a more than generous profit on the gold. He also knew that if there was an ounce of gold in the pouch, there was easily closer to four pounds than three. Realizing that his profits were about to walk out the door, he quickly spoke up.

"Let's not be hasty. Let me take another look. Perhaps I misjudged this a little. Mmm, I could maybe go say…"

"Twenty an ounce, and you weigh it this time! Now make up your mind. I've got things to do."The cold blue eyes were like icy daggers. Looking into them made the other man feel chilled to the bone. He knew that he had pegged James all wrong. Even so, he would make a healthy profit even at twenty dollars per ounce.

"Twenty it is. Let me weigh it out." As he transferred the gold to the scales, the assayer thought of one more possibility to get richer quicker. If he could find out where the claim was, he could file on it himself, if that had been neglected. Thinking he might just pull it off, he ventured the question. "Where did you find such a rich claim?"

James knew why the question was asked, so he enjoyed answering it honestly. "I didn't stake any claim. This was a gift from some friends of mine, Two Bears and Grey Cloud. You're more than welcome to go ask them where they found it if you want."

The townsman's face blanched, and he forgot all about trying to find out where that gold came from.

When the gold was weighed, it came to three pounds nine ounces. "Make it an even thousand dollars and I'll be on my way," Jim said. He knew that he had estimated low on the weight, but he didn't realize how low. The thousand dollars was more than he had expected and would last a long time if he was frugal. "Cash, and if anyone follows me from this office, I'll be back, after I've settled with them."

Jim headed straight for the bank where he deposited most of his cash. Carrying that much cash for too long was asking for trouble. Keeping two hundred dollars for supplies and traveling money, Jim began preparing. He had six excellent horses, a good rifle, and an exceptional knife, but he would need other supplies for his quest. Food, white man's clothing, for when he was in town, pistols, and plenty of ammunition were at the top of his list. The other thing he needed was information.

Remembering something that his father had said about barbers being a great source of information and knowing that he would need his hair cut if he were to be considered respectable, his next stop was the barber shop. While the barber cut two years of growth from Jim's brown hair, he talked and Jim listened. "You'll hear a lot more if you listen than if you talk," his father had told him, and so he listened now.

The barber cheerfully talked to Jim as if they were old friends. Information about range conditions, the weather, the upcoming barn dance, and more was passed along. Most of it Jim filed away in his mind as interesting and possibly useful, but when a stranger riding a certain dappled gray gelding with four white stockings came up, Jim was all ears. The description of the dappled gray with four white stockings and a white mane and tail sounded very familiar. One of the outlaws who had raided the ranch had been riding just such a horse. Seevers was his name.

"That sounds like a one of a kind horse to me," Jim stated. "I wonder if the owner would be willing to sell. What did he look like?"

"I don't know if he'd sell, but you never know. You can find him over at the Bon Ton. He's about five foot ten with coal black hair, a handle bar moustache, and a goatee. Real thin fella with some pock marks and a scar on his left cheek. He's riding with a guy that's missing his right arm. You can't miss 'em."

The barber finished, and Jim paid him and walked out. That barber sure had an eye for details, and Jim had found two of his family's killers in the first town he rode into. He'd see them very shortly.

Strolling down the street toward the Bon Ton, Jim spotted the dapple gray. Seeing the horse again left no doubt that this was the one ridden by Seevers. The sorrel belonged to Gates, the man who had lost his arm to Jim's father's bullet.

Stepping up to the batwings, Jim looked inside. He searched the room for any other members of the gang that might be present and let his eyes adjust to the dim interior before entering. Seevers and Gates seemed to be the only two outlaws present. Pushing through the doors, Jim glanced around one more time before speaking.

"Seevers, Gates, drink up and enjoy. It's your last one this side of Hell. You butchered my parents and sister and put the whip and hot coals to me. Today you pay."

The two spun around to see who the speaker might be. Seevers recovered first and went for his gun. The space between the combatants cleared instantly as Jim's rifle began to spout flame and lead. The first bullet shattered Seevers's wrist and the second one smashed Gates's remaining elbow. The next few seconds were filled with the sound of gunfire as Jim emptied his rifle into two men who were part of the group that had taught him to hate. The two knew terror as they were shot full of holes by someone they thought they had killed two years before. They knew terror, and then death, and then the flames of Hell welcomed them to their final destiny.

Almost before the echo of the shots died away, the town marshal arrived on the scene. He was a man of about fifty. Thick through the shoulders without much fat on his body, Marshal Tubbs was tough, confident, and competent. He was also carrying a ten-gauge express gun, just in case somebody doubted his authority.

"Just lay that Winchester on the table, boy, and have a seat." The voice held the ring of command. Running that thought, the fact that his rifle was empty, and that the voice was behind him left him only one option: comply.

Putting his now-empty rifle on a table, Jim took a seat with both hands in plain sight. He waited as the peace officer picked up the rifle and stood before him.

"What's this all about?" he demanded. "I didn't like those two either, but that doesn't mean I can just shoot them on sight."

Jim looked at the dead men on the floor. There were still six left, including Jacobs. If he was going to make them pay for their crimes, he had to stay out of jail himself.

"I'm James Harding, and those two are part of the gang that murdered my father, mother, and sister two years ago. Before they left the ranch, they gave me a parting gift as well." Standing slowly so that Tubbs would not mistake his actions as hostile, Jim turned his back to the marshal and carefully removed his shirt. Several people let out startled gasps as the scars on Jim's back were revealed. When he turned to face Tubbs, the livid marks left by hot coals burning his flesh were exposed as well as the scars of more than one bullet wound.

"Fourteen of them attacked my home. Six of them never left. Now that those two are gone, that leaves six including the ringleader. I don't know where the Wyoming and Montana boundaries are, so I guess I figured like the Old Testament says, 'An eye for an eye.'"

"Nobody can blame you for how you feel, son," began Tubbs. "Especially seeing how they left you after killing your family. The problem is that here in this town we don't take too kindly to gunfights. If this happens in my town again, I'll run you in for murder. Am I clear?"

"Yes sir," Jim replied. "My father was Dan Harding, and he taught me not to buck the law. What about outside of your jurisdiction?"

"Out there they fend for themselves, but be careful you don't cross the line and become one of that kind of animal. I knew of your pa, and it would grieve him if you did." Marshal Tubbs ended the inquiry and began ordering the removal of the outlaws' bodies.

"Marshal?" it was Jim speaking. "Their horses are out front, and their families should get their belongings. Gates is the fellow with one arm. Seevers is the other one. That's about all I know of them. I only saw them once before today." Jim had put his shirt back on and had picked up his rifle.

"You only saw them one time before today and that was two years ago? You remembered them that well from that long ago?" asked the marshal.

"My father taught me how to memorize faces and horses. What they did to my family and me burned their names and faces into my mind forever. I know all of them including their leader, Ben Jacobs. I won't forget them, Marshal."

"I reckon not," the lawman replied.

Jim pushed back out through the batwings and headed for the gun shop to begin picking up his supplies. First on his list was ammunition since he was nearly out. He also wanted at least one good pistol, maybe two. After that he would hit the dry goods store and get some "white man's" clothing, beans, and other staples for the trail.

At Dade's Shootin' Shop Jim found himself surrounded by a huge array of firearms for such a small town. He ordered three hundred rounds of 44.40 ammunition for his rifle before continuing.

"What do you have in the way of sidearms?" Jim asked. "I'd like .44 or .45 caliber, and I want something sturdy. Nothing fancy, just a good handgun."

When the proprietor looked dubiously at Jim, Jim promptly produced some of his cash from a pouch on his belt. That started a parade of pistols that would make your head swim. Remington, Smith & Wesson, Colt, Spencer, Hopkins & Allen, Iver Johnson, and more were shown to the young man at the counter.

Jim picked up several of the weapons to test them for feel, weight, and balance. His father had taught him how to handle a pistol as well as how to judge quality. Several weapons were handled and put back into the cases as just not feeling right. Others were pushed aside as being too heavy or too light. After about forty-five minutes of looking, only two boxes and a few used pistols were left. "I sure hope that you find something to your liking soon. I'm about out of inventory," the storeowner quipped.

Jim picked up one of the used Colts. He liked the feel and balance of the gun, but the front sight had been filed off and there were some pits in the barrel. The previous owner had taken poor care of it. After testing the few remaining used guns, Jim opened the two remaining boxes of new handguns. In each box was a pair of finely crafted pistols. Both pairs instantly drew his attention to the superb weapons.

The first was a brace of bone-handled Smith & Wesson forty-fours. Jim tenderly lifted them from their case. He tested them for weight, balance, feel. The Smith & Wesson felt very good in his hand. The balance was excellent and the weight was right. They were the best choice so far.

In the other box was a pair of Colt Peace Makers in forty-five caliber. While not as fancy as the Smith & Wesson, the polished cherry grips fit his hands as though made special, just for him. The single action worked smooth as silk and the weight and balance felt perfect to him. This pair of pistols would serve him well.

"Sorry to be so fussy. I'll take these," Jim indicated the matched pair of Colts, "and six hundred rounds of ammunition for them. Do you have a set of holsters for them too?"

"Sure thing. You ain't planning on starting no war with all of that ammo are you?" joked the shopkeeper.

"No. I plan to finish one," was the deadly serious reply.

No further questions were asked as the total was added up. The pistols were more than Jim had planned on, but the time would come, again and again, when he would be glad that he had spent the extra money.

"That'll be ninety-two dollars and thirty-eight cents," smiled the shopkeeper.

Jim counted out ninety-five dollars and waited for his change.

While the clerk was counting back his change, Jim asked, "Where is the best place in town to get supplies? I need clothes and some food for traveling. I've got a bedroll and some blankets, but I could use a coat and some gloves too. That, and is there some place to test out these new pistols?"

"Johnson has a better selection of what you might need, but Miller's stuff is a little less money. His food seems to be a bit fresher too. You can try them Colts out at a little spot just west of town. It's not a proper firing range, but that's where most of the folks from town practice," replied Dade. He was thrilled with the sale that he had just made and was more than willing to help this young man out.

"To Millers it is then. Thanks for your help." Jim collected his package and headed out the door.

Millers Mercantile carried everything Jim needed. He picked out some extra blankets, pants, shirts, a heavy coat, gloves, and a new hat. Dried beans, a slab of side pork, canned peaches, flour, sugar, coffee, and a few more items filled his order. Jim made arrangements to pick up the supplies the next morning. He took a pair of pants, a shirt, and his new hat with him. He didn't plan to stay in town long but could see no reason to sleep on the ground this night.

Jim retrieved his extra mounts and brought them to the livery barn to have them stabled for the night. After making sure his horses would be well cared for and grained, he took his packages and his rifle and headed for a nearby hotel. He had waited two years to get on the trail of his families killers. One night in town to rest wouldn't make any difference.

Five

The clerk at the hotel greeted Jim with a disgusted look on his face that suggested that Jim was beneath his dignity. "If you're looking for the flop house," he began with a nasally voice, "that's at the other end of town. We don't take no accounts that can't pay their bills here," he sniffed.

"How much is a room and a hot bath?" Jim asked. He was trying hard to resist the urge to yank the clerk over the counter and teach him some manners.

"It's three dollars for the room and one dollar for the bath, cash in advance," responded the clerk with an air of superiority. He seemed to think that would end the interruption of his afternoon reading by this white man in Indian attire and turned back to his newspaper.

Jim slapped five dollars onto the counter and growled, "I'll take both. I have some errands to run, but I'll expect my room and bath to be ready when I return. I'll leave some of my belongings here for safekeeping. If they have been disturbed or disappear, I will hunt you down to explain it. Now give me my key."

Looking into those glacial blue eyes, the clerk gulped. "Yes sir," he whined. How he had ever thought that he could run roughshod over this young man he wasn't quite sure. "Your belongings will be safe here. We run a very respectable establishment."

"By trying to chase away cash customers? I meant what I said. I'll return in an hour or two. Have the bath ready in two hours."

Jim took his key and his change and headed for his room. Once there he removed the Colts, holsters, and ammunition from his package of purchases and loaded both pistols before unloading and cleaning his rifle. The cleaning was done quickly and without fuss. He had learned from a very young age to take care of his belongings. The cleaning of his rifle, even if he had only fired one shot, was second nature to him.

The holsters that he had purchased would do for carrying the pistols but would have to be reworked or replaced if he wanted to be able to draw even reasonably fast. For what he had planned they would not do. First chance he had he would get a rig made to fit his needs.

He had changed into his new clothes but still retained his beaded belt and skinning knife. The rest of his Indian attire and weaponry would remain in his room until he returned. Jim took up his new hat and headed out the door toward a little café he had seen on his way into town. It was early for dinner but he was hungry, and there was no law against eating early.

The diner did not have a lot of patrons at the early hour, so finding a seat was no problem. The waitress was a pleasant, smiling woman in her late twenties. Her raven black hair was tied back revealing a strong tanned face and dark brown eyes surrounded by long black lashes.

"We don't have lots of fancy fixins, but what we have tastes good. We've got bear, moose, and even beef in stew, as roast, or as steak. They all come with biscuits with fresh honey, and fresh spuds. We even have a great blueberry pie if you want." She poured a cup of coffee for Jim as she waited for his order.

"It's been quite a while since I've had a good beef roast. How about that with all of the trimmings? If I have room after that, I'll take a big slice of that blueberry pie."

The waitress took his order. She returned shortly with a huge platter piled high with roast beef and potatoes. On a second plate were fresh baked biscuits still warm from the oven. A small jar of honey was placed on the table with part of the honeycomb still intact. The food definitely lived up to its billing.

As Jim was trying to decide if he had room for that piece of pie or not, there was a commotion in the street. He glanced out the window curiously. What he saw was a burly miner trying to kick a scruffy-looking mongrel and a skinny little boy of about six or seven doing all he could to stop it. The sight was almost comical as boy and dog defended one another against the grown man. It was almost comical, but not quite, for the miner was in earnest.

Jim hated to see children or animals mistreated and was out the door and in the street as the miner slapped the little boy to the ground and kicked the dog viciously.

The mousy-colored dog crouched beside the boy and growled menacingly at the man as he moved toward them.

"I'll learn you to let that cur run loose in the street and bother honest folks. After I'm done giving you your whipping, I'm gonna kill and skin that mutt of yourn."

The boy scrambled up from the dust and stood defiantly with his tiny fists clenched for battle. "Pepper ain't no cur. He's as fine a dog as any around. If 'n my pa were here, he'd teach you a sure lesson."

"Well, he ain't here now is he?" The miner sneered.

"Joey!" It was the waitress yelling as she raced out of the restaurant and to the boy's side before he could return to battle. He was determined to defend his little dog no matter what. Turning to face the miner, the waitress continued. "When Tom gets home, he'll hear about this."

"By then your boy will have learned some manners and I'll have a nice Pepper skin rug. Now step aside or I'll learn you too!"

The miner started forward again and a silver flash struck the ground within inches of his foot. The keen edge of Jim's bone-handled knife sank deep into the earth and the miner stopped instantly. He peered from the knife to its thrower.

"You're going to need a good skinning knife if you plan to take the hide off that dog. He looks pretty vicious. Downright tough, I'd say. That blade has a keen edge if you think you can use it." Jim's voice was soft as a rose petal, but his blue eyes were as hard as iron and as cold as a glacier. "Just be careful you don't get cut yourself."

"This ain't your business," growled the miner. "Why you butting in?"

"What's wrong?" taunted Jim. "Is somebody over the age of six too much for you? Or maybe the knife's too sharp?"

Furious,the miner bent and yanked the knife from the ground. He turned on Jim, which was exactly what Jim had expected.

"Maybe I'll teach you to mind your own business before I start in on this pair," he snarled, jerking his thumb in the direction of Joey and his mother.

40

The miner was at least twenty pounds heavier than Jim's one hundred fifty pound frame, but Jim carried no fat and had been training in some kind of hand-to-hand combat since he was about Joey's age. The last two years with the Cheyenne had only served to hone his skills and sharpen his reflexes.

He seemed completely at ease and perhaps a bit careless as he stood with his thumbs hooked in the three-inch wide beaded belt around his waist. He seemed at ease, but he was wound up as tight as a ten-day clock spring. That spring came uncoiled as the miner came at him with the knife.

Unfastening the simple catch on the belt, Jim slid it from his midsection and lashed out with it striking the miner's knife hand. The beaded belt might not seem like a weapon, but the beads were made of pieces of bone, hoof, metal, and antler. They were held together with tough sinews and many of the hard beads carried jagged edges. In Jim's skillful hands, it was all the weapon he needed.

The hard beads raked across the back of the miner's knife hand tearing furrows into his flesh causing him to drop the knife. Instinctively, he clasped his injured hand in his left hand and felt blood flowing from the injury.

"I told you to be careful not to get cut," Jim taunted. "I guess you should listen better next time. Now, I would suggest that you apologize to Joey and his mother and go have that hand looked at."

Looking down at his injured hand, the miner's expression changed from shock to fury and he charged in once more. Sidestepping the miner as easily as a matador sidestepping a charging bull, Jim struck again. This time the belt caught the trailing foot of his antagonist causing him stumble and fall headlong against a water trough.

Scooping up the razor-edged knife, Jim pounced on the back of the hapless miner like a cougar on a yearling doe. Drawing back the miner's head with a fist full of hair, Jim pressed the blade against the soft exposed flesh of his defeated opponent's throat. Leaning close he whispered to the miner, "I'm going to suggest, one more time, that you apologize to Joey and his mother before I decide to get mean. I've spent two years with the Cheyenne, so I know how to make a miner scalp rug if need be. Am I clear?"

The miner swallowed hard realizing just how easily he had been defeated.

"S-sorry, Mrs. Beechum. I'll not give you or your boy no more trouble."

"Apology accepted, Mr. Caruthers," replied the woman.

"Now apologize to the boy too," Jim growled. He pressed the knife blade against the miner's throat a tiny bit more, drawing a small trickle of blood.

"I-I-I'm sorry, Joey. I reckon I was outta line."

Joey's mom prodded him slightly. "Sure thing, Mister Caruthers. I suppose I forgive you."

Pepper had moved between the Beechums and the downed Caruthers. He moved forward tentatively, sniffed the miner's hand, and growled slightly before trotting back to Joey's side with his tail wagging.

"It looks like the apology is accepted even by the dog, Mr. Caruthers." Jim rose to his feet. "Be glad you didn't hurt the boy or his dog. I would have hated to have to make a miner scalp rug my first day in town."

Turning to the waitress and her son he continued. "Ma'am I do believe that I've worked up enough room for that blueberry pie now, but only if this fine young man will join me for one of his own. I believe that a boy who will stick up for his friends deserves a big slice of pie at the very least." Jim was smiling as he squatted down in front of the little boy and scratched Pepper's ears. "That is, if it's all right with your mother."

"Of course," Joey's mother stammered, "but how can I charge you after what you did for my Joey?"

"I'll be insulted if you don't let me reward his courage and loyalty. Too many grown men are lacking both."

After the pie, Jim ordered coffee for himself and a big glass of milk for Joey. He enjoyed the excited chatter of the little boy, and when he let it slip that he had lived with the Cheyenne for two years, Joey's curiosity went into full swing.

"Are they always on the warpath? Do they really scalp women and children? Can they really ride on the side of their horses?" These questions and more poured from the excited child.

"Slow down a minute," laughed Jim. "For the most part they're folks like you and me. Their beliefs are different, but they have good and bad just like white folks. They teach their children to respect their elders and they honor courage and loyalty. They make good friends and really bad enemies. Of course, whoever heard of a good enemy?" They both laughed. "I suppose they know nature better than we do, but that's what they've lived with all along. Now how about you? Where did you get such a fine animal as Pepper?"

Joey beamed with pride as he talked about Pepper. "He was the runt of a litter of pups out to one of the farms. My pa was hunting a cougar that had been killing some of their stock. Well, pa, he killed that big cat as dead as a doornail and when he brung it in to the farm as proof. He said that Pepper was the onliest pup with enough spunk to take after that cat even though it was already dead. He told that farmer he'd take less than agreed to if 'n he'd throw the pup in. Pa told me to teach him right and he'd be a good friend."

"Well, your father sure knows how to pick them. That Pepper is one to ride the river with. I don't believe I've seen a finer dog anywhere."

After a little more conversation, Jim paid his bill and asked for a big soup bone for Joey to give to Pepper. "He deserves to be rewarded for his loyalty and courage too," he explained.

Jim headed back to the hotel to get some sleep before heading out the next morning. The hotel clerk had followed through on his instructions and had the hot bath ready on time. After his bath Jim slept soundly and didn't notice the rider heading out of town like the Devil himself was chasing him during the night.

Early the next morning, Jim loaded up his supplies and found his way to the makeshift shooting range on the edge of town to get accustomed to the new revolvers. After burning up several loads of ammunition, he felt somewhat comfortable with his new weapons. He passed back through town just long enough to have a good breakfast and bid his new young friend farewell.

He gathered his spare horses, loaded the rest of his supplies on one and headed out of town. Circling wide of town, he hoped to pick up the trail of the two most recently expired members of Jacob's gang and backtrack them to the rest. His father's training supplemented by the two years with the Cheyenne made him far above average as a tracker. To backtrack someone who wouldn't have been trying to hide their tracks shouldn't prove too difficult for him. If the gang had remained intact, he might find them very soon. Unfortunately for him, a heavy storm had passed through after the two had reached town and washed away any sign that might have proven helpful.

Jim spent the next several days searching for any sign of his family's killers but found none. After finding two of his intended targets so quickly, he was disheartened somewhat by his lack of progress. Still without a real direction to resume his hunt, he decided to return to his home and visit the graves of his family. Maybe that might prove to be a good place to begin his quest anew. Besides that, he really wanted to see his old home once again. He knew it was silly, but he was homesick.

 Six

H e had come into town for a drink. The talk at the bar was all about a shootout earlier that day. He listened with only half interest. Stories of gunfights were interesting, but in the west they were not all that uncommon. Halfway through his second drink something in the story caught his full attention. The two that had been killed in the gunfight sounded very familiar. In fact they sounded a lot like Seevers and Gates. They had taken off almost a week before to spend their proceeds from the last job.

Listening more closely to the story he learned that the man that had killed both of them wore Indian attire but was definitely a white man. He had icy blue eyes and had called both men by name before opening fire. When he inquired about the identity of the shooter, nobody seemed to remember his name, but they all gave a fairly accurate description other than adding several inches to his actual height. The scars and the cold blue eyes were unmistakable.

Unable to glean more information, the traveler had a few more drinks before making his decision. Gates and Seevers were dead, and the boss had to know about it. He hadn't been with Jacobs as long as the others but knew that these two had been with him since the beginning. Exiting the bar he mounted and thundered out of town heading back to the outlaw camp. It was well past midnight when he took his leave from town.

"Jacobs."

"Yeah, what do you want? And where are Gates and Severs? I thought I sent you to fetch them back!"

"They ain't coming back," was the truculent reply. "They's dead. Near as I can tell, they was having a drink when some stranger comes in, calls them by name, says something about his family, and empties his Winchester into them. Cut them to doll rags. Some that saw it said he just laid his rifle aside when the marshal arrived and took off his shirt. He was covered with scars."

"Said something about his family? Scars?" Jacobs was thinking out loud. "It can't be. He's dead." He turned his attention back to the other man and continued his inquiry. "Anything else they mentioned?"

"His eyes. They said they was blue and cold like a glacier. Said he was wearing Injun clothes too. You know, buckskins, leggings, moccasins, and such, but he was sure enough white. Talked real good they say."

Jacobs felt a slight shudder run down his spine like someone had just stepped on his grave. "If anyone asks, they got killed in a gunfight but nothing about this stranger. I need to do some thinking on this."

If young Harding had survived, but no, that was impossible. No man could survive what he had been through, and someone had put two more bullets into him just to make sure. It had to be a coincidence. It had to be.

Seven

He rode into the ranch yard expecting it to be overrun with weeds and in need of repair. Instead he saw a ranch beginning to grow once again. His father had built the ranch with the intention that it continue long after he had gone to his reward. Even so, it would not happen if nobody was there to work and maintain it. Someone was obviously working it.

Jim's eyes narrowed and he clenched his teeth. Someone had moved into his father's home and taken over. They had taken what they had not worked for and what was rightfully his. He kneed his horse closer to the house and swung quickly from the saddle, rifle in hand.

He was greeted by a double warning. A rifle cracked and a geyser of dirt erupted near his feet. That was one. The second came in the form of a feminine voice. "Stand where you are or mount up and ride off." His anger had initially made him overlook the flowers planted near the stoop, but he noticed them now. They weren't stealing this ranch, someone was making it a home. His mother would be pleased.

His anger began to abate. "Mind if I put my rifle away and water my horses, ma'am?" he asked. "It's been a long ride."

"Put the rifle away and water your stock. I might shoot you, but I won't deny your animals water. There's a pump…"

"By the corral next to the barn." He finished the sentence for her and started that direction leading his horses.

Two pairs of eyes watched him as he operated the hand pump filling the water trough for his horses. "Are those Indian ponies?" asked the owner of the younger set of eyes. The eyes were large, brown, and set in the round face of a pigtailed girl of about six. Her freckled face was split by a wide smile of wonder that displayed the gap waiting for her front teeth to grow back in. She stared at the man in wide-eyed wonder. He was the first visitor in a long time and her natural curiosity was running wild.

"I don't know, Sarah," her mother responded. "Some might be, but they all look to be fine animals and very well cared for." She had noticed the horses with the eyes of a frontier woman. They were cared for without being pampered. "We'll have to wait and see what he has to say."

"Okay, Mommy. Mommy, when I grow up, will I be as smart as you?"

Her mother laughed. "Smarter I hope, sweetheart." Her laughter reached her own brown eyes, and she watched the familiar way the stranger moved around the ranch yard. No misstep nor uncertainty about where things were located. It made her a little nervous that someone should know the layout so well. Had he been watching from hiding? A cloud moved over her face and she shuddered slightly. Thomas would arrive any minute and know what to do. He would have heard the shot and would be on his way.

Since there were no other animals in the corral, Jim walked to the gate and led his horses into it. It was a bit presumptuous, but he did still technically own the ranch. That had been in his father's will. He was certain of that.

He loosened the cinch on the horse he had been riding and removed the bit from its mouth before putting a nosebag on him and each of the other horses. When he had finished that task, he walked slowly to where Two Bears had buried his family. There had been no markers on the graves, other than a large pile of stones, but he knew which one held whose body.

As he rounded the corner of the barn and approached the graves, he noted that they had been neatly trimmed and someone had planted a dogwood near the head of the center grave. He knelt at the foot of the graves. "Ma, Pa, Rachael. I don't know why this happened and I don't know exactly how or when, but they will pay," he said between clenched teeth. Tears had sprung up and he dried his eyes before standing.

"Did you know them?" Little Sarah had slipped quietly from the house and approached him silently.

Startled, Jim spun pulling his right hand Colt as he did. Sarah's mouth dropped open in astonishment and she began to cry.

"I'm sorry," Jim said, quickly holstering his pistol. "You shouldn't sneak up on folks like that. In answer to your question, yes, I did know them very well. They were good people and didn't deserve what happened to them."

"I helped Daddy plant the dogwood tree," she said quickly, recovering from her shock. "Daddy says it has the cross of Jesus in the blossoms every spring." She smiled her toothless smile. "I'm Sarah. What's your name?" From tears to smiles in less than a minute.

"I'm Jim." He extended his right hand to her and enveloped her small hand in his. "It's a pleasure to make your acquaintance. And now you should…"

"Sarah!" The feminine voice from earlier that had held so much command, was now almost in a panic. "Sarah!"

Sarah dashed toward her mother. "I'm right here, Mommy, talking to Jim. He knows the people in the graves."

Jim walked toward them. "Don't be too hard on her, ma'am. She seems very well mannered and she was just being curious, like little girls are."

Three riders swept into the yard. A man with a strong jawline riding a huge chestnut stallion led the way. He leapt to the ground and stood beside "mommy" bristling. "Dinah, what was that shot? Is everything all right?" He asked her the question but faced Jim like a lion defending his mate.

"Thomas, I'm so sorry I got you all worked up. It was a warning shot I'm not so sure was all that necessary. Then Sarah sneaked out and I couldn't find her and I panicked. But she's right here now."

"Here I am, Daddy. I was talking to Jim. He knows the people in the graves."

Thomas's eyes narrowed. "How did this stranger know who was buried in those graves?" he wondered.

Not more than five feet five inches tall, Thomas carried a lot of bulk in his chest and shoulders. Coal black hair framed his strong face and his hazel eyes danced with fire as he stood in defense of his family. He wrapped a protective arm around Dinah.

His bride stood no more than five foot tall and had large brown eyes like her daughter. The two had married when she was young and Sarah was born a year later. Dinah was just beginning to show signs that she was carrying their next child. Her long brown hair was tied back revealing a smooth expressive face.

"Okay, who are you?" Thomas demanded.

"He's Jim," Sarah offered before Jim could speak for himself.

"You told me that, sweetie, but that doesn't tell me *who* he is."

Jim proceeded cautiously. Anyone could make the claim he was about to make, but, in his case, it was the truth. "I'm James Harding, and I own this place. The people in those graves are Daniel, Ruth, and Rachael Harding. My father, mother, and sister. I appreciate you planting that dogwood by their graves. Ma would have liked that."

"You're who? And you what?" growled the black-haired man. His rifle tilted menacingly toward Jim and he stepped away from Dinah. "I was told this place was abandoned. Now you ride in here out of nowhere and claim it's yours. I'll ask you one more time. Who are you?"

Jim gritted his teeth. He was covered by at least three guns and his anger would serve no purpose here. "I already told you. I'm James Harding, sole surviving heir of Daniel and Ruth Harding and the owner of the Lazy H."

The two men's eyes locked. There was challenge in both men's eyes. Tom's seemed to blaze with fire and mistrust while Jim's turned icy cold.

"Stop it!" Dinah's voice broke the spell. "Thomas, please. Maybe he's telling the truth. He knew right where the graves were. He knows who is buried in them, and he knew where the pump was. Please, let's hear him out."

Tom took a deep breath and slowly released it. He and Dinah had longed for a place to call home, and just as they had begun to build that home, some stranger shows up to claim their home as his own. He had better be able to prove it, or there would be trouble.

"Okay. Let's talk."

The tension had begun to dissipate but did not completely leave as Tom led the way into the house. Sarah took Jim's hand and pulled him along behind her into the house. For some reason beyond adult reasoning, she trusted him. "Daddy's mad at you," she whispered to Jim.

"I kinda noticed," Jim whispered back.

Waiving Jim to a chair, Tom took a seat across the table from him and glowered. Dinah brought both men some coffee and biscuits left over from breakfast. "Sarah, honey, why don't you go outside and play with your dolly for a bit while we talk."

"But, Mommy, I wanted to—"

"Go now." Dinah's response was gentle but firm.

Sarah reluctantly picked up her doll and headed out the door. She could be heard talking as she went out the door. "I know, Molly. He seems nice to me too. I'll introduce you later when they're done being grownups." Her voice faded as she took Molly to see the horses in the corral.

Dinah smiled at her daughter's words, "when they're done being grownups."

Jim interrupted her thoughts. "Ma'am, you surely do have a sweet daughter there. She's quite bright."

"Thank you, Mister Harding," she replied guardedly.

"Now that Sarah's outside, what's this all about? We've been here over a year, and this is the first we heard of anyone else laying claim to this place. How do we know you are who you say you are and not some thief with a slick story?"

Jim tried to place himself in Tom's shoes. How would he feel if the tables were reversed? What would he think? As best as he could, he recounted the story of his last two plus years with the Cheyenne. He did not leave out the killing of Gates and Seevers. "The trail turned cold, and so now I'm back here where it all started." He ended his narration and walked to the fireplace. "I know it sounds far-fetched, but it's the truth. Two of the horses I have wear the Lazy H brand. I know that doesn't prove anything, but…" Jim shook his head slowly.

"So yours is the missing grave," Tom stated solemnly. "They said there were four that lived here, but there were only three graves. Most figured you had been dragged away and killed by the Cheyenne. I suppose you'll be wanting us to move along now." His voice was low and husky. He hadn't shed a tear since he was ten and his grandmother died, but his eyes were moist. The thought of having to move somewhere and start again with Dinah five months along and all they had tied up in fixing up the Lazy H weighed on his broad shoulders like a grand piano.

"I hadn't thought that far ahead," Jim admitted. "I never really expected to find anyone living on the place, especially a family." He scowled. "I take it that means you believe I'm who I say I am?"

"Yeah, you're him. The missing grave and the Injuns calling someone they found 'Can't Die.' I should have known this day would come. We'll start packing in the morning if that's soon enough for you."

Dinah had sat in her husband's lap and held his hand. She knew how much having a home for her and Sarah meant to him, and now that dream seemed to be crushed and him along with it. *Not in front of a stranger*, she thought, but the tears flowed of their own accord. He pulled her to him and stroked her hair lovingly.

"We'll be all right, honey. We have each other and Sarah."

"Don't start packing yet. I need some time to think this through." Jim walked to the door. "I'll sleep in the barn tonight. I'm going to scout around the next few days for some things my father may have left. I'd take it kindly if nobody shot me." He turned and left the house.

Before dawn the next morning, Jim was saddling a pinto mare for his first foray to search for the gold deposits his father had found. There had been some clues but not many as to where it might be. Dan had passed some knowledge of geology along to his son. That, coupled with his knowledge of some of his father's habits, would help him, he hoped. To continue his quest he would need more money than what he had, and the gold was the fastest legal means he knew of to get it. That, or sell the ranch, which he could not bring himself to do.

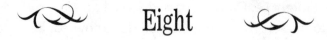

Eight

He rode out of the ranch yard to the southeast just as the sun crested the horizon. Tom and Dinah watched his silhouette disappear around the corner of the bunkhouse.

"He scares me, Tom."

"He wouldn't dare harm you or Sarah." Tom's voice was strong and reassuring.

"No, not that. I could see it in him when he talked yesterday. Like a wounded animal or a wolf on the prowl, or maybe a bit of both. He wouldn't hurt us, but he's hurting. Do you mind if we pray for him this morning? I saw his eyes when you two faced off yesterday. They were cold, almost dead."

"Did you hear that, Little Tom?" he said to her belly. "Ever the mother trying to help even an injured wolf."

She punched him playfully in the chest. "Thomas Bartholomew Dalton!"

How could he resist her? He pulled her gently to himself. "Yes, my dear. We shall pray for your injured wolf. We will pray that Mister Harding's eyes and heart will soften. And that he won't kick us off this place. It was meant to be a home."

Unaware of the attention he was attracting, James was deep in thought. He couldn't run the ranch and hunt his family's killers. "Maybe the..." He had failed to get their last name the previous evening. Maybe they could run it for him leaving him free to pursue Jacobs and his cohorts. It would give him a home base to work from and provide at least some income.

With that settled in his mind he swung back to the west passing within a mile of the house. He was searching for something, but he wasn't quite sure what. A marker or clue but what exactly he had no idea. His father was never gone more than a day and sometimes less than that when he went to his gold field. It had to be within just a few miles of the home, otherwise he would not have been able to make the trips so quickly.

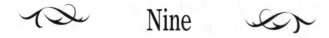

Nine

arah stretched and yawned. Rubbing her eyes, she carried Molly with her to the main room of the house. "Good morning, Mommy. Good morning, Daddy." She yawned again and snuggled close to her mother to watch the sun rise.

"Well, good morning to you, Chipmunk. How is my little angel this morning?" Tom's eyes beamed with adoration as he looked down on the product of his and Dinah's love. Soon they would be blessed with a little brother or sister for Sarah. He smiled and placed his hand on Dinah's slightly swollen belly.

"I'm sleepy, but Molly is hungry, so we got up. Can we help you make breakfast, Mommy?"

"Of course you can, sweetie. Why don't you go get dressed and we'll fix the men, and Molly, something to eat."

Tom smiled as he watched her skip to her room with Molly tucked under one of her arms. "She favors you, my dear, which is good for her." He rubbed a hand across his stubble-covered chin. "It'd be hard for her to find a man if she had a face like mine and had to shave regular like." He winked at his bride.

"She's only seven!" Dinah scolded. "She doesn't need a man right now except her daddy, and he's required to love her, beard or no beard." She kissed her husband on his unshaven cheek and winked at him playfully.

Sunset found Jim riding back into the ranch yard aboard a leg-weary mount. He had travelled many miles searching while never really venturing more than a few miles from the house. While he did not find what he was searching for, he did see that Tom had begun cutting hay against the winter even though it was still early summer. He had planted some of the irrigated acreage with grain and fruit trees. Tom obviously knew how to work and was planning on this becoming a home. An idea that had started in his mind earlier began to take shape. Rubbing down the tired horse before turning her into the corral, Jim thought the idea through and made his decision.

Tom and Dinah were sitting on the front porch watching the moon rise and noticed the thoughtful attitude of the young owner of the Lazy H. "Good evening, Jim. Did you find what you were looking for?" Dinah asked.

"No, but it can't be far. I'll find it soon. I'd like to talk to you about something, if I may."

"You haven't eaten all day. You must be starving," Dinah stated. "Let me get you something to eat."

"I had some hardtack, but if it wouldn't be too much trouble."

"Come in and sit," Tom invited. "Dinah can scare you up some stew and we can talk while you eat."

The stew was thick and hearty. Jim ate quickly. He pushed his chair back. "I've been knocking around an idea in my head all day. I don't know you, but I can see you've been working hard here to make this place a home and make a go of it. My father built this place to be a home. I don't think, after what happened here, it can ever be that to me. At least not the way he meant. But I do need a place to come back to and rest. I plan to bring those who slaughtered my family to justice."

"How?" Dinah asked.

"I plan to hunt them down like the dogs that they are and see them dead, by my hand or the hangman's noose. I don't rightly care which."

Dinah blanched but remained silent.

"Anyway, what I need is someone to care for this place while I'm busy. Someone who might make it a home yet. What I am proposing is a partnership of sorts. You provide the work and run the operation, and I provide title to this land, several thousand acres, and the stock that was once my father's. After expenses we split the profits fifty-fifty, but I retain fifty-one percent control. Is that fair enough?"

Tom and Dinah exchanged a shocked glance. Their mouths hung open for a second or two. They had been fearful of being kicked off the ranch they had thought of as home. Instead they were being offered a partnership in what Tom predicted would be a cattle and horse empire.

"Well, umm yeah, that's more than fair." Tom rose and extended his hand to Jim. The men shook and the deal was sealed. Dinah just nodded mutely. Tears again filled her eyes, but this time they were tears of joy and relief.

"Thank you," she whispered.

"I'll ride into Longbow tomorrow and have the papers drawn up so nobody can dispute your claim."

 Ten

rue to his word, Jim visited his father's attorney to have the papers drawn up. Arthur Bollinger was a man now close to sixty, but not a man to be trifled with. He was straightforward and honest in his dealings and his advice. When Jim walked into his office, Arthur's jaw dropped and the papers he was sorting through fell from his fingers to the desktop. He stared, bug-eyed. "Jimmy, I mean, James, is that really you? We all thought you were dead for sure! Where have you been?"

He raised his lanky six-foot three-inch frame from the well-padded leather chair. Finding his way around the desk, he extended his hand to shake. His long fingers still had a powerful grip as they closed around Jim's hand.

"Well, I'm not dead yet," Jim replied. "I've been here and there, and now I'm back. There were some squatters on the place when I got back."

"Do you need a notice to evict them?"

"No, nothing like that. I actually have a different thought and need some help putting it together. You see, it's a family, and they've been doing a real fine job on the place." Jim quickly recounted his story ending with finding the Daltons on the ranch and outlining his idea. "So, any advice?"

"Some, but you're more stubborn than your old man was, so you won't listen. Even so, you asked for it, so I'll give it."

"The business deal sounds like it is workable, but you're giving up half the profits from the ranch. Of course, you will be sharing the burdens too, so it works out. If they've been there for a year, it might be easier and more beneficial than trying to kick them off the place, especially if he's as industrious as you seem to think!

"As for the other, leave them to the law. They will get their reward in the end. That's the part I think you'll ignore. If you insist on hunting them down, stay inside the law, don't shame your folks by crossing over. Remember, vengeance is a hollow goal.

"So are you ready for me to write up those papers for you? I'll even ride out with you to see the place and get the necessary signatures tomorrow if you want."

It was late afternoon by the time Bollinger finished the paperwork. While Bollinger wrote up the papers, Jim visited the local leather smith to have him design an appropriate gun belt. That was something he wanted before he went back out on the hunt. "Do you want it cross draw or regular?" the leather smith asked. "I know some prefer the cross draw, but I think when you draw it straight up, you get a better shot than when you swing it from side to side, but that's your call."

"Let's not use a cross draw. My father never liked them much and neither do I. What do you need from me to get started?" Jim asked.

"Let me see your guns and I'll get some measurements on you. That'll give me some preliminary stuff to start," the leather smith stated.

"How long will it take to make? I'd like to get a feel for it as soon as possible," Jim asked.

"It will take a few weeks to get it set just right. I can put one together quicker than that, but not for what you got in mind." The leather smith was a grizzled oldster with experience in everything from saddle, to boot making, harness repair, and making exceptional holsters. "Son, I'll make the rig for you, and you won't find a better one anywhere. It'll be custom-made for you, but I know what you want it for. I can't say I blame you, but remember, revenge is a dark master. It'll eat your soul if you follow it too far. Don't let it drag you down to Hell."

Jim listened to the admonition. "Just make the rig," he said. He surrendered his guns and holsters and submitted to the measuring.

"If you're still in town come morning, you can have your guns back. I'll have my blocks made up by then."

"Thanks, Mister Cosworth. I'll come by tomorrow and pick them up before heading back to the ranch."

"The price you'll pay for this rig won't be cheap, and I ain't talking about the money, although that won't be cheap neither. You get a reputation as a fast gun and there's those that will look for a fight just to prove they're faster."

"I'll be careful of that. I had better let you get to work or you won't get finished."

Jim stepped back out of the leather shop. The clean Montana air washed the smell of curing hide and leather from his nostrils and lungs. Some people liked the smell of a leather shop. He preferred the smell of hay and pine.

He returned to Bollinger's office as another client left. "It looks like you keep busy."

"Hey, Jim, I was just finishing up for the day. I have your partnership papers drawn up. Why don't you let me buy you dinner tonight? You're paying for it anyway." The attorney laughed. "We can go over the paperwork while we eat. I can file it for you when I get back to town tomorrow afternoon. We'll need to make sure your father's will is enforced too, but that won't be hard. In a couple days we'll have it all wrapped up."

"Sounds like a good idea to me," Jim responded,

After the deal was signed, Jim spent the next few weeks divided between searching for his father's claim and visiting Cosworth's leather shop. Each visit to the leather smith found the gun belt closer to completion but Cosworth was not completely happy with it. He would again measure, adjust, and mutter about how it wasn't ready to try yet. He'd then send Jim off for a few more days while he made the corrections.

It was during one of these interludes between visits that Jim spotted it. It was a marker his father had taught him as a small boy, three limbs on a small tree were pulled together and tied pointing in one direction. It was something that could be easily missed unless you were looking for it. He followed the direction it pointed. A half mile later he almost overlooked the next marker. It was four white stones arranged like an arrowhead just off the path he was following; it was pointing in a completely different direction.

Pushing his horse through the brush, he came to the game trail that wound close to the face of a stone ledge leading to a shallow stream with a sandy bottom. Several large boulders were strewn across the stream, which disappeared into a crevice to reappear, most likely down closer to the ranch house. In fact the house was only about five miles away, but completely blocked from view.

Riding to the stream, Jim dismounted to let his horse drink. Glancing at the sand bottom where it appeared that animals were fording, Jim noticed a glint in the bottom of the stream. Squatting for a closer look, he noticed the sandy bottom of the stream seemed to be mixed with a golden glitter. He took a handful of sand and let the water wash the lighter sand and silt from his hand. Flecks of gold stuck to the lines in his hand. It had to be washing down from somewhere higher up. His father brought in nuggets as well as dust, but this was a good start. He may find nuggets just up the stream, in the eddies behind the large boulders in the stream, or buried deeper in the sand bottom.

He took a gold pan he had carried with him from the house and waded deeper into the stream. Scooping up a pan full of sand, he swirled water in it washing the sand from the pan while the heavier gold flecks remained. There was a small amount of gold in the pan after his first scoop. He decided to move farther upstream and picketed his horse on thick grass growing near the crystal-clear creek.

Moving against the current, he waded to the nearest boulder and panned gravel from near the base of it. Finding a little color here and there, he continued to work his way further and further from the game trail that crossed the creek. Rounding a bend, he spotted a ribbon of ragged quartz that had split, dumping tons of the crystalline stone into the edge of the creek and exposing a mineral formation spider-webbed with the soft precious metal he sought.

With his mouth agape, he walked to the pile of rubble and sifted through the heap picking up ore that he could literally dig the gold out of with his knife. He had found his father's claim, and as rich as it was, it was no wonder he had kept it a secret. If word leaked out and it wasn't properly guarded and worked, claim jumpers would arrive in droves destroying the landscape and more than likely draw in the usual lawless crowd that followed boomtowns. Jim knew his father would never have wanted that.

Taking what he thought would be sufficient for his immediate needs, Jim headed back to the ranch by a circuitous route. He would need to figure out what to do about the gold, but for now it would remain a secret. It was surrounded by land he now owned, so it should remain safe, he hoped. He would talk to Arthur Bollinger about his options and how to protect his range from those who would surely try to find the deposits. Mr. Bollinger was a knowledgeable man in such matters.

"I'm going to be riding out soon," Jim stated that evening after dinner. By this time he had become a regular fixture at the Dalton dinner table. "Not real sure exactly when or for how long, but I'll be back. I'm going into town tomorrow for a few things before I leave. Is there anything we need? I can take the buckboard and pick up supplies while I'm in town."

Tom and Dinah worked with Jim to compile a list of things that were needed for the ranch. When they finished, Dinah asked, "Where are you off to?"

Jim's eyes hardened and he set his jaw. "Unfinished business," he stated flatly. Dinah started to say something else, but Tom cut her off with a shake of his head. They both had an idea as to what the unfinished business was. From the look on Jim's face, Tom knew that there was no changing his mind.

The next morning Jim hitched up the buckboard and headed for town. Stopping at the general store, he gave the proprietor the list of supplies and said, "I'll be back shortly to load up." He walked to Bollinger's office.

Arthur was seated at his desk riffling through some legal papers when Jim entered the office. He glanced up and smiled when he saw who it was. "Good morning, Jim. To what do I owe this unexpected visit?"

Jim withdrew a leather pouch from his belt and sat it on the desk. "I found my father's diggings," he stated. "I need some advice. I know he wouldn't want the countryside all torn up or swarming with people digging holes all over our place. It's rich and is on land I hold title to. It would be good to develop if it can be done without destroying the land. I figured you would have a better idea about how to handle it than I would. Maybe there are some legal issues too?"

Bollinger let out a low whistle when he opened the pouch. "I'd keep this quiet for the moment. Let me check some things. If it's on your land, it should be safe. You may need to file a mining claim, but for now you should be okay."

"If you wouldn't mind checking on that I would appreciate it greatly," Jim responded. He trusted Arthur's judgment. "I've got another stop or two to make while I'm in town. I think I'll exchange the gold somewhere other than here though. I have sufficient cash for my needs today. I don't want folks searching the land while I'm gone."

Nodding his head, Arthur said, "That's a good idea, the fewer people with any idea where it came from the better. You said something about being gone. Are you planning a trip so soon after returning?"

Jim responded, "Yeah. I have some unfinished business. I will be heading out as soon as Cosworth is finished with my rig. He said it should be done today when I was in the last time. It'll take a couple days to get used to it, but then I'll be riding out again. "

Bollinger gave him a knowing look. "Don't you think you should let the law handle it?"

"The law has had two years. I think it's my turn. You know what the Bible says, there is a time to kill and a time to heal. I'm pretty much healed, so I guess it's time for the other." Jim stood and started for the door. Turning he said, "I appreciate all you've done. I will be back and then we can discuss what you found out about filing a claim."

Jim stepped out onto the boardwalk and started for Cosworth's. He pushed aside any questions Bollinger's comments might have raised in his mind about his chosen course of action and thought instead about the brutality of those he would soon be hunting. Thinking of his family, he steeled himself for the task ahead. If the law wouldn't do the job, he sure enough would!

Waiting for Cosworth to finish waiting on a cowhand who had ordered one of his famous "Saturday Night" saddles, complete with exceptional tooling and some inlaid silver, Jim remembered his sister Rachael and her courage as she fought for her home. He also remembered the man who brutally rode her down. His reverie was broken when he heard the cowboy exclaim, "That's well worth the four month's pay it cost me!" He watched as the puncher almost reverently picked up his purchase and carried it to his waiting mount.

"He's right, Mr. Cosworth, that sure was some saddle."

"Aw, 'tweren't nothing much. A little tooling, some silver, and a lot of polishing. I think he'll enjoy it, though. Now for you, my young friend."

Cosworth reached under his workbench and drew out an oil cloth-wrapped package. Laying it on the counter in front of Jim, he said, "It's all finished. Unwrap it and take a look." Jim opened the oil cloth and lifted the belt from its wrappings. Unbuckling the holster he was wearing, he swung the new rig around his lean waist. The brown leather gun belt wasn't ornate but did carry the Lazy H brand on the belt just in front of the right-hand holster. It had Cosworth's initials stamped into the belt as well. A craftsman always signs his work, and Cosworth was a craftsman.

Tying the holsters down with the pigging strings provided, Jim unloaded his pistols and slid them into their new receptacles. In one fluid motion he drew, cocked, and dry fired his right and then his left-hand Colt. While snug, the holsters did not inhibit the swift withdrawal of either six-gun. After a few dry runs, Jim reloaded his weapons and filled the loops in the new belt with the cartridges from the old belt. He smiled as he shelled out the agreed upon price. "They are better than I expected."

"They're the best I've made," the leather smith smiled. "Just remember what I told you before."

"I will, but I'm remembering my family too. I'll see justice done even if it's with these guns. Thanks for the rig and the advice." Jim turned and walked out into the bright midmorning sunshine.

He strolled back to the general store. Finding the order had been pulled during his brief absence, he paid the bill and with the help of the clerk loaded the buckboard for the ride back to the ranch. Noticing some stick candy, he thought of Sarah and bought three of them for her. Tucking them into his pocket, he turned the wagon toward home. His last stop on the way out of town was a small stone structure.

Jim halted the team in front of the marshal's office. He jumped down and walked through the door. A middle-aged man with a slight paunch, bald head, and handle bar moustache looked up as the door opened. His bored expression changed as he noticed Jim's tied down guns. He was new to the area but not to young men with two guns. "Yeah," he growled. "What can I help ya with?"

"Marshal, I'm James Harding co-owner of the Lazy H. What I'm seeking is information on a gang of cutthroats and murderers."

"There ain't such in my town," the older man snapped.

"Marshal, I never figured they were here. If they were, you'd be planting them or seeing to their hanging. They won't come back here."

"Okay, now we got that established, let me give you the what-to-for. First, I'm marshal here, and I won't stand for no gunplay in my town by you or nobody else, so don't be telling me I'd be planting anyone. You'll keep them hog legs holstered in my town. Second, I don't give information to man hunters just on their say-so. Now, I'll ask again, what can I do for ya?"

Curbing his first instinct, Jim struggled to remain calm. He had only stopped to make an inquiry, not to try to buffalo the marshal. "I already told you, Marshal, all I'm looking for is some information on some wanted men. You're new here, so you might not know what happened at the Lazy H a couple years ago, but I was there. The men I want are responsible for the murder of my parents, my sister, and darn near myself. If it wasn't for the Cheyenne, I'd be dead too. I figure I'm alive to see justice done, if I can find the rest of them."

"I'm listening."

"I'm searching for a man named Jacobs. He ran a gang that included Wolfe, Gates, Severs, Tanner, and several others. I found Gates and Severs. I'm just wondering if you've heard anything from your flyers about them or their associates."

"You're hunting them that killed your family, huh? Well, that is some different. I heard of a bunch that might be them, was involved in some robbing and killing over toward Scott's Pass and Ketchum Springs way. We got a wire about that few weeks ago. A stage got robbed going through the pass. That feller Wolfe killed a gambler when he reached for his gun. That gambler was s'posed to be quick, but he for sure is dead. You could ask the sheriff over that way for information. He might could help."

"Much obliged, Marshal. I'll be heading out that way in a day or two."

Taking his time, Jim arrived back at the ranch in time to unload the wagon and clean up for dinner. Sarah skipped to the wagon with Molly in tow. "Hi, Jim. Did you have fun in town? Daddy says sometimes Kenny and Pete have too much fun in town, but they don't look happy when he says that. Jerry just laughs at them." Jerry was an older and wiser hand.

Jim laughed. He could just guess the kind of "fun" that Tom was referring to. "I had a nice ride, and as soon as I get this wagon unloaded, I have something for you and Molly, as long as your mommy doesn't mind. As a matter of fact, I have one for her too." He pulled the candy from his pocket. "There's one for you, one for Molly, and one for your mommy. Ask her first and don't eat it before dinner."

Her big brown eyes widened and she smiled showing her teeth just starting to grow in. "Wow, thank you, Jim, and Molly says thank you too!" She ran to the house to show her mother the candy.

"I'll be riding out tomorrow," Jim announced after dinner. "I've got a lead on the men I'm after. I'll take that paint mare for a packhorse and that roan gelding to ride. Use the others here for ranch work. If you sell or trade any of them, keep that buckskin. He's had some special training, and I'd be hard-pressed to replace him."

"How long will you be gone?"

"I'm not sure, Dinah. I guess, expect me when you see me."

"You can't go, Jim. Molly will miss you. Who else would buy her candy?" Sarah's lip quivered and her eyes misted.

Jim smiled. "I've got to go, Sarah. There are some really bad men I have to find. They do some really mean things, and I think I'm supposed to stop them."

"But the sherriff can catch them and make them stop."

"The sherriff can't go where they are, and nobody else will do it. It's something I have to do. They're the ones that hurt the people in those graves. I have to go. Don't worry, though, I'll be back."

"Do you promise?" she sniffed.

"Of course, I promise."

"Jim, you could leave it to the law to handle." Tom knew he was wasting his breath, but he had to speak.

"They've had more than two years and haven't handled it yet. It's up to me to see that they get what they've got coming." His voice was like a rasp running across hard board.

"We'll miss you," Dinah said softly.

Eleven

The next morning Jim rode purposefully to the southwest. If he travelled steadily, he could make Ketchum Springs in a few days. There he would talk to the local law, if they would help. At least now he had a more recent sighting of those he sought. The few days on the trail would also give him a chance to get accustomed to his new holsters. He'd brought plenty of ammo for practice.

Trotting his horse down the main street, Jim looked over the town and its residents. It appeared to be typical of the mining and cattle towns in the area. False-fronted buildings lined the rutted street. Only a couple of them sported any more paint than was needed for a sign. The residents were a mixture of townsfolk, cow punchers, and miners all going about their business.

He drew a few stares on his entrance to town. He was dusty from the trail, but his gun belt was clean of all but a slight film. Tied down holsters were sometimes seen but rarely two, and Jim's face held a grim expression. His horses were exceptional stock, far better than the usual cowpony. He had the look of a hardcase as he swung down in front of the saloon.

"Got coffee on?" he asked the bored bartender, after sweeping the dim interior for potential enemies. He had never acquired, nor did he want to acquire, a taste for alcohol.

The bartender poured a cup of steaming brew. "Want I should add a dollop? We got real Kentucky for two bits."

"Just coffee. I like to keep my head clear when I'm hunting. You seen any new faces in town?"

"Why, sure I have, youngster. There's one right now drinking coffee and confabbing with me. He, he, he. And he don't want no dollop of good Kentucky Bourbon in it neither. Now that is new if 'n ya ask me." The bartender laughed again. "I reckon the only way it could be any newer would be if you asked for that new sody pop stuff. Sarsaparilla they calls it. I got some in on the next stage after the hold up."

Jim turned his cold eyes on the bartender. "Anyone besides me," he growled.

Unaffected by the hard gaze directed his way, the man responded."Well, why didn't you say so? Not any so you'd notice. At least not for a month or more. Any one in particular?"

Jim gave a short concise description of the men he knew of that might be riding with Jacobs. "You got an eye for detail. You a lawman?"

"No, they just gave me plenty of reason to remember them. I plan to return the favor. If they have forgotten myself or my family, I'll remind them."

The man thought for a moment. "I don't recollect any of them, but they may have passed through."

"If you happen to hear anything of them, I'd take it kindly if you would pass the word along. My name is Harding, and I'll be around for a day or so." Finishing his coffee, he dropped more than enough to pay for it on the counter and walked out. He had doubted that he would find them here in town after the robberies, but he didn't think it hurt to make inquiries. He would make a point to stop back by the saloon before he rode out of town. Maybe he would try that, what did he call it, Sarsaparilla.

He mounted and rode the one hundred yards to the assayer's office. After his last encounter, he was ready for a repeat of the events. Instead he found a smiling man in his late twenties ready to deal with those who exchanged minerals for cash.

Jim pulled the pouch containing his dust and several nuggets he had found in the stream, and the pocket of quartz. It was not quite as heavy as that which Two Bears had given him, but it was a goodly amount.

"It looks like you found yourself a pretty good claim." The assayer smiled. "Let me get my scales and weigh it out. I might not have the cash on hand for it, but I can write a check for you that you can draw from the bank. Most men don't bring in this much at a time. "

After checking the gold for quality and weighing it, the assayer scowled slightly. "There's a little bit of stuff mixed in, but this is pretty close to pure. I don't keep that much cash on hand, but the bank will honor my note if you don't mind."

"As long as the price is fair, I've no problem with that."

The price was quickly negotiated and Jim headed to the bank with a note for several hundred dollars in his breast pocket. The money would carry him for several months of his hunt. He didn't think it would take that long. He told himself as much, but his prediction proved to be in error. The hunt would not prove as easy as he hoped, nor would it end as he planned.

After collecting his money, Jim visited the sheriff's office. A tall angular man with a clean-shaven face, which was darkened and wrinkled from exposure to the sun and wind, was pouring over wanted posters. The town's new arrival was on none of them. Glancing up he saw the face he had been searching for in his pile of dodgers. While he had not expected to find Jim's face on any of the posters, neither did he expect to find him standing in his office.

"Is there something I can help you with?" The lawman took in the twin guns worn by the lean, hard-eyed young man in front of him. He had noted him when he rode into town and watched as he made his stops around town. It was his job to know who was in his town and any newcomer drew his immediate attention, especially one who, to his trained eye, had the look of a hard man, even if he was young.

"I'm looking for information," Jim responded. "I heard there have been some holdups in the area. I believe they may have been committed by some people I'm trying to find. I heard they may be working between here and Scott's Pass. At least that was the word I got from the marshal back home."

"What are you looking for them for?"

Jim briefly explained. "I figure to find them and see justice done. The trail is a couple years old. If it's them who have been plaguing the area around here. That gives me a lot fresher trail to start on."

The sheriff gave a few minutes thought before he answered, "I can tell you where they've been operating and where we lost their trail, but I can't help you more than that."

"That's all I could ask for. Not to worry, I'll be riding out as soon as my horses are rested." Jim had read the sheriff's concern about public safety in his bailiwick correctly and saw the relief on his face at that announcement. Not that Jim struck him as a trouble hunter, but he believed that he would not shy from it either. He also knew Jim was carrying a good sum of money and that naturally attracted evil men. (He had inquired of the assayer after Jim left for the bank). Sheriff Denton gave Jim directions and saw him out.

The next morning, after a hearty breakfast, Jim checked on his horses and decided they would do well with another day of rest. He stopped at the general store to replenish the supplies he had used on his ride to Ketchum Springs. While there he purchased four boxes of forty-fives and another box of forty-four Forty's for his Winchester. "Is there anywhere around here that a man can shoot off his guns that won't cause a ruckus?" Jim asked as he picked up his purchases.

The proprietor directed him to a copse of trees a short way from town. "Plenty of young fellers go there to improve their aim or to try to impress their friends with how fast they are. Most couldn't hit a barn from the inside with their fire-arms, but they try." He chuckled as if it might be the voice of experience.

"Thanks." Jim smiled and walked out the door. After depositing his purchases in the stable with his pack saddle, he threw his saddle on the roan and rode leisurely in the direction that the shopkeeper had given him.

For the next few hours Jim burned through cartridges. Setting up targets of old cans found on the ground or sticks and a few bottles, he drew and fired from varying positions, each time trying to shave a split second from the last and striving to make each shot hit the chosen mark without conscious thought.

"You is mighty quick."

Jim spun to face the speaker. He had just emptied his right-hand Colt and had not had a chance to reload it. He had been so absorbed in his practice that he had failed to notice the soft approach of the person whose voice had startled him. Facing him was a large black man carrying a machete in his right hand. The sinister, curved blade was naked in the sunlight.

"Now if you'd be so kind, I'll takes your money you done got from da bank. I know that gun you be holding is empty."

"I don't think I'll be that kind nor will I give you anything."

"Din, I'll just takes it offin' your dead body."

Bringing the machete up, he advanced menacingly toward Jim.

Jim's right-hand Colt plunked into his holster as his left was drawn and pointed toward the thief. Jim hesitated but the negro did not. As he swung his weapon in a downward arc, Jim fired, slamming the would-be thief and murderer two steps backward. The heavy forty-five caliber slug smashed into his breastbone. Pieces of rib bone and the now-flattened bullet shredded heart and lung and the assailant flopped to the ground. His arms were flung to the side and his sightless yellow-rimmed eyes stared out of a flat face into the sky. His soul found a place reserved for one who lived by brutality deep in the blackness and eternal flames of Hell.

Jim punched the spent cartridges from his right-hand Colt and reloaded it before doing the same with his left. He would have to report the killing, but there was nothing else he could have done other than let himself be killed. He was mad clear through. He should have noticed the approach long before his assailant was that close.

He stalked to his horse and swung astride. Pointing his horse toward town, he started for the sheriff's office at a shambling trot. "Might as well get it over with," he thought.

The sheriff was out, but a man acting as deputy took Jim's statement and rode out with him to where the body was. The deputy stopped at the undertaker's along the way. He followed shortly with his wagon to retrieve the body.

"Everything appears like you said. I recollect seeing him skulking around the livery. Looks like he found more than he bargained for. I'll let the sheriff know you rid the world of some trash. You're free to go."

Jim figured that even though the killing was justified, his welcome in Ketchum Springs was worn out. He decided to stop by the saloon and try that "sody" pop the bartender mentioned before eating and turning in early. His horses would be rested, and he planned to be up and gone before the sun rose. The bartender didn't have any information for Jim, but he enjoyed his sarsaparilla anyway.

Twelve

unrise found Jim miles from town riding southwest toward Scott's Pass. He planned to set up camp a few miles from the pass and scout the area on foot. While riding horseback would be faster, it would also make him more visible and leave more signs for those he was hunting to discover. A horse would also limit his possible routes of travel.

Turning off the stage route, Jim rode into a canyon he had spotted about a half mile from the trail. He wasn't too worried about anyone following him, but he still took precautions to make his trail less obvious. A little caution never hurt anyone. He didn't want his hideout to be easily discovered.

Jim's eyes never stopped moving as he rode into the confines of the canyon. He scouted the mouth of the canyon, finding the tracks of deer and coyotes. He saw no sign of human travel. Farther up the canyon he found what he was looking for. A pool of clear water was fed by a small spring gurgling up from between a few boulders. Surrounding the spring was a cluster of trees and several acres of lush green grass, watered by the spring. A small herd of deer bounded away at his approach indicating that no other humans were close by. From here, he would be able to do his hunting unobserved.

He set up camp under the trees, but back far enough from the pool so animals could come to drink. The position was invisible from the mouth of the canyon and defensible if need be. It was perfect for what he intended. After unpacking and picketing his horses, Jim opened the map he had acquired from the sheriff and began to plan.

Jim spent the afternoon and early evening examining the map for trails to and from the stage road. He knew that not all of the trails would be found on the map, but he thought why not check those that were marked first. The locations of the holdups were clearly marked on the map. His father had taught him to think a problem through and that was what he spent the next hours and days doing.

Trying to put himself in the place of those he hunted, he thought of escape routes, hiding places, and so on. Using the map, he quickly eliminated several trails as too heavily travelled or too far from the holdup locations to be practical. He had reduced the possible routes and camp locations considerably by the time he rolled into his blankets for the night.

For the next two weeks he was up and moving before dawn. Never taking the same route twice, he scouted the area for the outlaw camp. He hid his trail and only returned to his own camp after dark to avoid his own hiding place being discovered. He scouted the main stage trail by horseback but moved on foot when checking any of the trails that might be the route taken by the outlaws. He was better able to approach those trails unseen in this fashion. His moccasined feet helped aid in his silent vigil. They also left much less of a trail.

A lone rider on the stage road caught his attention on the fifteenth day of this search. The rider was unfamiliar to him, but knew well where he was going. He turned off onto a game trail and returned to attempt to mask his passing. Waiting for the rider to disappear from view, Jim thought his luck had turned.

Slipping silently back to where he had hidden his horse, he mounted and returned to his hidden canyon. He would cut across country from there on foot in order to follow the trail.

Unlike most cowboys, Jim didn't mind travelling on foot. When stealth rather than speed was essential, it was his preferred mode of travel. Saddles creaked and iron spurs could easily strike a stone sending a warning to anyone in the area. He wore a buckskin shirt and brown trousers that would blend with the dried grass and dust.

Thinking on what weapons to take, Jim decided on something out of the ordinary, at least for a white man. Taking a fur-wrapped bundle from his gear, he withdrew a powerful Cheyenne bow. At fifty yards he could put five out of five deadly arrows into a five-inch circle. The bow was strong enough to kill a bull buffalo at that range. None of the animals he was hunting were buffalo. At seventy-five yards, it was more than enough to kill a man. It also had the advantage of being almost silent.

Taking the bow and a quiver of steel-tipped arrows along with a water skin and some jerked beef, Jim set off at a lope across country. Alternating between the lope and a fast walk, he covered the distance to the game trail in a minimal amount of time. He also did so without stirring up dust, which he would have had he been on horseback.

Now he settled down behind some brush to let his heart slow back down and to study the trail. He had no desire to be caught in the open while checking for tracks. After waiting and watching for about thirty minutes, Jim slipped out along the trail to study the tracks in the dusty ground. Mixed in with those of several mule deer and some antelope were the tacks of the rider he had spotted earlier. Any older tracks had been wiped out by the passage of time.

Paralleling the trail, Jim traveled undercover stopping regularly to listen and watch. At dusk he had made about four miles along the trail. He knew their camp had to be near and stopped for the night. Having no desire to alert them of his presence, he made a cold camp and settled in to wait out the darkness.

As night fell, a faint hint of smoke touched his nostrils. He smiled. They must feel secure to have a fire. He made plans to change that.

Testing the faint breeze, Jim picked up the light odor of burning wood. He rose and moved as silent as a shadow upwind. The scent of wood smoke grew stronger and he soon picked out the flicker of firelight in the clear night air. It was a new moon, so the only light was from the stars and the campfire.

One careful step after another Jim slipped stealthily toward the camp. Circling the fire he watched for sentries but saw none. About a quarter mile from the camp Jim settled down to watch. He had located the horses and remained crosswind from them to avoid them alerting the camp. The night was cool and clear. With the new moon, all was dark but that which was illuminated by the fire. Jim could make out the figures around the fire and counted nine outlaws. Jacobs had brought in more men.

In his inspection of the camp, Jim had verified that these were the men he sought. He recognized the blue roan that one of the raiders had ridden during the attack on the ranch. He also recognized Wolfe's Appaloosa in spite of the limited light.

Watching the lackadaisical way the camp was set up and guarded, or rather not guarded, Jim devised a plan and smiled to himself. Setting his plan into motion, he snaked his way slowly toward where the horses were picketed. When still a little way from the first horse, he rose slowly to his feet in the shadow of a large bush. The camp was quiet by this time. Whiskey and the late hour had taken effect, and the outlaws lay sprawled around the dying fire wrapped in their blankets.

Talking quietly to the horses, Jim moved among them cutting their picket lines. He moved them slowly away from the camp. Jim led the captured horses for the first mile then mounted one of the horses and trotted for another several miles. Then, turning them all loose, he started them off into the fading night and turned back toward his own camp.

The sun was up, and Jim was dead tired by the time he arrived back at his own campsite. He led his horses to water and then picketed them on fresh graze before rolling into his blankets for a few hours respite.

It was late morning before the outlaw camp began to stir, but the shout of alarm shocked all of the outlaws into complete wakefulness instantly. Guns in hand, they dove for the surrounding brush but found no enemy present. Jim was already miles away resting safely in his own hideaway. It would be another hour before he stirred from his slumber to put the next step of his plan into action.

"I told you we should have set a lookout," one of the outlaws grumbled. "Now what we gonna do? You can't rob no stagecoach on foot!"

"Whatcha think we're gonna do, you nitwit? We're going to trail them horses and hang us a horse thief," growled Jacobs. The irony that they themselves were thieves was completely lost on him and those around him. "There's no sense all of us trailing after the horses. Gonzalez, you, Mickey, Abbott, and Taggert follow the horses." Jacobs ordered Taggert to travel with the others since he was the one grousing about the night guard. The others were the best ropers in the gang.

Taking the two lariats left in the camp, the four trudged off following the trail left by the departing horses. The twelve horses, including the packhorses, left an easy trail to follow.

High-heeled cowboy-style boots, like those worn by the men, made walking difficult, and the terrain the horses were taken through led deeper into the rough country. Hours later they had yet to sight the horses. It was hot and dusty, and the four outlaws had grown tired and irritable.

After sleeping for a few hours, Jim rolled out of his blankets. He saddled his horses and packed what supplies he had. Removing as much sign of his camp as possible, he mounted and rode off to intercept the party he was sure would be trailing their horses on foot. He grinned as he thought of what the outlaws were going through. He only hoped that some of the search party were the ones he was seeking. By this time they should be plenty footsore and on edge.

The sun had passed its zenith when he spotted the four searchers. Their cursing and complaining made locating them a simple thing. If there were any hostile Indians nearby, all he would have to do was watch. Jim knew that was not the case. His intended victims did not.

Leaving his horses hidden from the route the outlaws were traveling, Jim slipped into position to intercept them. Hidden some sixty yards from the trail left by the horses, he hunkered down to wait. He decided against the use of his rifle since the bow he carried would serve more than adequately and might cause even more alarm than a rifle shot. The cursing, grumbling men moved into bowshot and paid little heed to their surroundings. Nocking an arrow, Jim let it fly from his hidden position. It struck slightly lower than the intended mark, but the effect was no less dramatic.

The arrow struck Taggert in the hip joint, tearing cartilage and shattering the shaft to leave splinters imbedded deep in his hip and thigh. Taggert spun and fell as the shattered shaft ripped his flesh.

"Injuns!" Abbott hollered, and all dove for cover waiting for the attack to continue. Taggert was left where he fell. Cursing the others for leaving him in the open, he crawled toward cover. Jim had slipped silently to another position. The next arrow sliced through Taggert's right forearm halting his crawl toward the nearest concealment.

The other three men poured lead blindly into bushes and possible hiding places with no effect. In a panic, one after the other turned and ran leaving Taggert alone with the attacker. Abbott had been in the raid but was out of bowshot before Jim could shoot.

"Don't leave me!" Taggert screamed at the disappearing backs of his supposed friends.

"Too late for that," he heard a voice state. The voice seemed to come from everywhere and nowhere. The voice also sounded somewhat familiar and yet he could not place it.

"You should have picked better friends," the voice taunted.

Taggert reached with his left hand toward his holster only to find it empty. His pistol had fallen from it when he fell after being struck by the hard-flung arrow. A chuckle sounded from near where his fallen Navy Colt lay. An apparition seemed to materialize from the tiny bit of cover near his pistol. It was a white man, and Taggert recognized him.

"No, it can't be. There's no such thing as ghosts."

"You're right on that last part, but it can be, and it is me. What's the matter, Taggert? Did you think I would break my word about seeing you hang?"

Jim picked up one of the dropped ropes and shook out a loop while Taggert tried to scuttle away using his good arm and leg.

"I should let you bleed out or die from infection, but I promised to see you hang." A loop snaked out from Jim's hand and settled around the outlaw's neck. Jim yanked it tight.

The spot for the ambush had been selected for more than mere convenience. Dragging his victim behind him despite the strangling noises, Jim tossed the coiled rope over a limb of the only tree nearby. Taggert's injuries made resistance impossible. "You slaughtered my family like dogs. This is better than you deserve, but like I said, I promised you a hanging."

Jim hauled on the rope and dragged Taggert erect. Then, placing his feet against the trunk of the tree, he hauled him off the ground. Taggert's face turned purple and his eyes bugged out as he kicked spasmodically trying to loosen the rope. His struggles only served to tighten the rope around his neck until they slowed and stilled and his tongue lolled out of his open mouth. With his injuries, he was unable to do anything but strangle.

"So long, Taggert. Enjoy Hell." Jim turned away. Before leaving, he shoved a note into the dead man's mouth. He thought this would bring a sense of satisfaction, but all he felt was revulsion. He steeled himself against it by remembering that this was one of the men responsible for the murder of his family including his little sister. Jim started back toward his horses leaving the gruesome figure swaying in the mild breeze. As he trudged back to the hollow where his horses were hidden, the figure of

Taggert haunted him. Each time it arose he remembered his family and forced his doubts aside and with them a little bit of his own humanity. By the time he swung into the saddle, his mind was cleared of any guilt. His conscience was being seared. He turned away knowing that he would be unable to surprise the party hunting the horses again. They would be alert and would shoot first and ask questions later.

Thirteen

inding that they were not pursued, the fleeing bandits slowed their panic-filled retreat and regrouped. "How come they ain't chasing us?" whispered one of the hardcases.

"Beats me," responded another. "I don't hear no war whoops. Maybe we should sneak back and take a look see."

"You go ahead. I don't figure to get my hair lifted."

"C'mon, we can't leave Taggert to them savages. Come to think of it, I ain't seen no sign of Injuns 'round here. Maybe it was just some lone buck. If 'n he killed Taggert, it would be good to send him over before he brings back some friends. "

Reluctantly, the trio began inching back toward the scene of the attack. Forty-five minutes later they spied a strange sight for what was supposed to be an Indian attack.

"Injuns don't hang folks, they scalp them." The tone was questioning.

Swiveling their eyes to search the area, the men stood erect and walked toward the still form. The three moved forward warily. "They sure enough hanged him. And with one of our own ropes," drawled Abbott.

"Them's moccasin tracks, but I'd bet you it weren't no Injun that strung Taggert up," stated Mickey emphatically.

"What makes you say that?"

"He ain't got his gun or knife, but there's still bullets in them loops. No Injun would leave them."

"What's that in his mouth?" asked Gonzalez. "I have never seen Indians shove paper into a man's mouth before, or hang one for that matter."

Having Mickey and Gonzalez lower Taggert's body to the ground, Abbott pulled the paper from the dead man's mouth. There was a message scribbled on the paper. "Hey, Mickey, can you make this out? I don't make much sense of them written words."

"Let me see it," grumbled the bearded man who had been addressed. Squinting, he worked his mouth as he read the message.

"Well?"

"Gimme a second! It says, 'I promised you all I would bring you to justice. I keep my word.' It's signed 'A ghost from your past.' He names them who was with Jacobs all along. That don't make no sense."

"Perhaps not, but Mister Taggert no longer is among us," observed the Mexican.

"Let's drag this body into the bushes and go get them horses." Abbott's orders were obeyed. After the body was covered with brush, the three continued to warily trail the horses. It was well past midnight before they returned with ten of the horses. The others were lost.

"Where's Taggert?" demanded Jacobs when the three rode dejectedly into camp.

"He ain't coming back," Mickey muttered.

"What do you mean?"

Abbott swung down and walked to the fire filling a cup with scalding coffee. He took a sip and looked across the fire at their leader. "Somebody done hanged him. This here note's for you I figure."

Jacobs took the crumpled note. "'A ghost from your past,' what's that supposed to mean?"

"I do not know, but this ghost must have flesh and bones because he used a rope to hang Taggert." The dark-skinned bandit smiled a little in the firelight. "Perhaps someone should make him a real ghost."

"Maybe so, Gonzales, but for now that stage is our target. After that you can hunt down this 'ghost' and make him one for real."

The talk turned toward the stage holdup planned for the next day. Until now, all of the robberies they had pulled had come off without a hitch. The only hiccup had occurred when the gambler had tried to draw on Wolfe. Even after that one, the sheriff had lost their trail and they were free to continue their trade along this lonely stretch of stage line.

Fourteen

The rattle of trace chains and the creak of harness leather let the outlaws know that their quarry was fast approaching.

The pop of the driver's whip over the backs of the horses urged them to greater effort as they pulled to the crest of the hill they were climbing. Once over the ridge, the driver would pull up to allow the team a blow before continuing on their way. There had been no sign of bandits or trouble so far, and the passengers might want to stretch their legs as well.

Pulling the team to a halt among some trees that offered shade, the driver jumped down from his perch. "If ya'll wanna stretch your legs, hop on out folks."

The shotgun guard remained on his seat scanning the area. He knew the horses needed a rest after the long uphill pull, but he still did not like to stop. He felt uneasy but could not see the reason for his unrest. When the last of the passengers, a young woman with dark wavy hair, stepped from the coach, a rope shot out of the tree line and dropped around the guard. His arms pinned to his sides, the man was jerked brutally to the ground. Several masked men with drawn weapons stepped from cover.

"Okay folks, I don't figure any of you are carrying anything worth getting dead over, so just put your money in the sacks my man is passing around. Driver, we'll take that express box you got too, and please don't try to grab that shotgun. It'd be a shame to mess up that shiny coach with your blood."

"Someone's coming, Boss," muttered one of the masked men.

"Nobody let on we're here and nobody'll get hurt. Get back into the brush." The bandits faded into the brush before the rider arrived.

Jim followed the stage line planning to alert the authorities of his findings in the next town. Seeing the stage stopped up ahead, he kicked his horse into a canter not realizing he was riding into a robbery in progress. His packhorse trailed dutifully behind.

"Nobody better warn him," hissed the outlaw leader. "Not if you want to see the sunrise tomorrow."

"Howdy folks," Jim called cheerfully. Then he saw their faces and knew something was wrong. He swung his horse and felt a heavy blow in his side. He swayed in the saddle and toppled to the ground. The last thing he heard before losing consciousness was a woman's scream and a voice he should recognize saying, "He's a ghost now." Then blackness overwhelmed him.

"Better make sure," ordered the bandit leader. As he pointed his pistol toward the supine body, the dark-haired girl stepped between them.

"He's already dead, you brute! Take what you came for and leave him be. Why did you shoot him anyway?"

"It was personal reasons. Okay, girlie, I don't reckon he'd be alive after that anyway. If he is, it won't be for long. Driver, get that box down."

One of the outlaws bent to search what he thought was a dead man and found Jim's money belt. "Whoeeee boys! Looks like this here was a bonus for us!"

"Throw that body in the coach and get this stage rolling," the outlaw leader ordered. The passengers complied glowering at the outlaws but powerless to do more.

After the stage rolled away, Jacobs turned to the man who had fired the shot. Pulling down his mask, he grinned. "I reckon you sure enough made him a for-real haunt this time, Keegan. Only I don't figure he'll be haunting us no more." The outlaws all laughed at the joke and fled the scene in a cloud of dust.

At the first lurch of the coach, a slight groan escaped Jim's lips. "He's still alive," exclaimed the girl. She quickly checked his pulse and found a very weak one. Tearing the shirt from the wound, she found where the bullet had passed through his body and stopped against the skin of his back. Swiftly she tore the hem of her petticoat and plugged the entrance hole. She tied the crude bandage in place and one of the male passengers hollered to the driver, "Get this coach rolling, this feller's still breathing!"

The pop of the whip and the shout of the driver brought a surge of speed from the six-horse team. The stage bounded along the road and the young woman sat on the floor cradling the head of the injured man. She valiantly tried to staunch the flow of blood, her face nearly as pale as Jim's. "He simply cannot die now. He can't!"

An older woman who had been traveling with the dark-haired young woman spoke, "Madeline Jean, he's hurt bad. He may not even make it another mile let alone to town where he can be treated. It is a miracle he is alive now."

"But he's alive, and God can still do miracles, can't he, Aunt Betty?" The girl was almost crying.

"Those are both true, honey, but I don't want you to be upset if this young man does not survive despite your efforts."

"I know. I just hate to think that anyone would die just for riding up and saying 'Hello.' It's just not right. "

Fifteen

The dire predictions of Aunt Betty did not come to pass on the trip to town. Halting the weary team in front of Doc Becker's place instead of the stage station, the driver and guard jumped from the box atop the stage and carried the limp body of Jim inside. The doctor hurriedly examined the patient and grunted. "He's closer to dead than alive, but I'll do what I can. If none of his insides are torn up too bad, and he didn't lose too much blood and I can get the bullet out without him bleeding out, he'll probably die anyway, but I'll see what can be done."

"Madeline! Madeline Jean!" A man's voice rang out through the crowd. Fear tinged the voice. He had seen the stage roll into town and stop in front of the doctor's office. In the swirl of dust and confusion, he had failed to see the young woman emerge from the coach. When he was informed she was with the doctor, he feared the worst.

Strongly built, though beginning to thicken around the middle, the man shouldered his way through the throng that had gathered. Gray had touched his temples, but his hazel eyes danced like flames as he pushed forward.

Erupting from the door, the petite young woman in question flung herself at the man. She threw her arms around him. "Daddy! Oh, Daddy, I'm all right, but they shot him, and I can't leave him alone!"

"Are you sure you're all right, honey? Who? Who did who shoot? What do you mean you can't leave him alone? Who is 'him'?"

Before she could reply, an older, slightly plumper version of Madeline moved breathlessly through the crowd. "Jeremiah, did you find her? Is she all right?"

"He found me, Mother, and I'm quite all right, but the young man in the doctor's office is hurt badly. I told the doctor I would stay with him until he wakes up."

"Stay with who?" her mother inquired.

"I asked her the same thing. Well, daughter of ours, would you care to enlighten us?"

Madeline quickly recounted the events of the holdup and the discovery that Jim was still alive. "He can't die, Mother. I'm going to sit with him while he gets better."

"He's not some baby bird that fell out of a tree, young lady, nor an injured puppy. You have no idea what kind of man he is, and from what I heard on the way over here, he's closer to dead than alive."

"Daddy, please, he's hurt and he needs someone. If he does die, he shouldn't have to die alone no matter who he is." Barely one hundred pounds she might be, but she had her father wrapped around her little finger.

"Cassandra, talk some sense into your daughter please!"

"Mother, Father, I am staying to help! I bandaged his wounds and I shall stay until he recovers!" She stomped her foot. She could be a spitfire.

"Very well," her father conceded, "but remember he very well may die, and he is a man, not a stray puppy or kitten. Some day he will rear up on his hind legs."

"Oh, thank you, Daddy." She threw her arms around her father's neck again. She then hugged her mother. "Thank you both. I know he will live. I can feel it." She dashed into the doctor's office.

Aunt Betty hurried from the opposite side of the coach. "Jeremy, Cassie!" Her eyes sparkled as she hurried toward them. "It was most awful! Dreadful!" Betty had come from the East accompanying her niece who had been to visit her in Ohio. "Those brutes robbed us at gunpoint and just shot that young man out of the saddle. It was dreadful, I say. Then your daughter spouts off at their leader like she was daring him to oppose her. That little snippet of a girl might have gotten herself killed for a stranger."

Jeremiah smiled slightly as his mind pictured the scene with his fiery little girl facing off against armed bandits. No doubt about it, he and Cassie had raised a spitfire, and they would have to keep an eye on her. Whatever man she set her cap for had best have some fire of his own.

His bride of almost a quarter century saw his lips turn upward and knew his thoughts. She knew him too well. "And what pray tell, Mr. Jeremiah Wendell Stark, are you thinking that puts such a grin on your face after our daughter has faced such peril?"

"Why, Cassie my love, I was just picturing your daughter facing down armed hooligans with nothing but her will and her tongue. She does so take after her beautiful mother." He winked.

"Now, Betty, shall we gather your luggage and get you settled? I have a carriage waiting at the station. When you are settled in, then I believe it would be wise of me to visit this injured 'bird' my daughter has taken upon herself to nurse back from the dead." Now that the fear for his daughter's safety had been relieved, Jeremiah's voice boomed in jovial exuberance.

"You jest, Jeremiah, but those ruffians may well have harmed your daughter. They were vicious I tell you!"

Jeremiah laughed out loud. "Betty, out here, even the most vicious of bandits who would kill a man for a few coins would not dare to harm a good woman, or any woman for that matter. The best they could hope for is a bullet or a rope, and they know it. I don't know what men are like in peaceful Ohio, but out here they respect women. Now if you will excuse me." He left the house to head for Doctor Becker's office.

"Why, of all the..." Betty stared after her brother-in-law, fuming for only a few seconds. Then she smiled. "He sure is proud of your little girl, isn't he? So was I, the way she stood up to those outlaws, but I was scared for her too."

"Jeremiah is right, though. Many a bad man who dared harm a decent woman has found himself dancing at the end of a rope, many times provided by their own partners. She was safe enough. Now let us go and make that meal. We have so much to talk about."

The doctor walked out of his operating room to find Madeline sitting in the waiting room. "Well, miss, your man is still alive, but I don't know how."

Madeline's pretty face turned crimson. "He's not my man, Doctor. I do not even know his name. I just thought that some-body should be here when he wakes up."

"You mean, *if* he wakes up, don't you, ma'am?"

"No, I mean when he wakes up!" she said forcefully. "I have to believe that if he survived the ride to town that he will recover. I have to believe that."

"Well, miss, you sure do put a lot of pressure on this old sawbones, but I've gotta be honest. He don't look good, and I don't expect he'll be here come morning."

"Can I sit with him, Doctor? If he is to die, he should not have to die alone."

"All right, but don't expect him to be taking you to any barn dances now or in the future. Crazy girl!" The last two words were muttered under his breath just as Jeremiah Stark arrived.

The muttered words were heard by Madeline's father. "Try being her daddy," Jeremiah responded with a wink.

Mister Stark quietly entered the room where his only daughter fidgeted. She would sit for a few seconds then stand and walk to the bed where her patient lay, bathing his forehead with a cool cloth. Her father smiled as he watched. So many times he had watched her nurse an injured animal or care for a baby bird that had fallen from its nest. Once, Madeline had even bought home a cougar cub whose mother had been killed by a local farmer when she had gotten into his hogs. Fortunately, a travelling animal act had come through town and took the cub off their hands before it got big enough to do more than kill a few chickens.

When she turned from fussing over the unconscious man, and saw her father watching, she exclaimed, "Oh, you startled me, Daddy! Where are Mother and Aunt Betty?"

"They went home to put together something to eat. You must be famished after your ordeal."

"I guess I am a little hungry, but I can't leave him here alone."

"Let's give them a chance to catch up and put together a meal. You and I can do some talking as well."

She smiled sweetly at her father. "It has been a while since you and I have talked, Daddy, but let's keep it quiet." She indicated Jim. "He needs his sleep."

Her father laughed out loud. "Honey, if our talking wakes him that would be more of a miracle than Lazarus being raised from the grave. But just so you don't worry, let's go to the other room and talk."

Two days later, Jim was battling a fever. He had not yet regained consciousness, but somehow Madeline had managed to spoon a little broth into him. Now his wounds were inflamed and he thrashed deliriously threatening to reopen them.

"Keep a cool cloth on his head, Madeline," Doc Becker instructed. "I've got to clean them wounds or the infection will kill him sure."

Doctor Becker removed the bandages and reopened the wound to let it bleed some to wash out the infection. Then he redressed it, shook his head, and left the room once again.

Night and day Madeline had stayed near her patient. The morning sun shined in the window behind her. Its warmth lulled her tired body and mind and her eyelids fluttered shut. Through the night Jim had raged with fever and delirium. His fever had broken the day before then returned, and last night the doctor had said if the fever did not break for good this time, then his patient would surely die.

She took the doctor at his word and had spent a sleepless night changing bandages and bathing her patient with cool clothes. "Just a little rest," she thought. The sunlight through the window made her hair take on a slight halo effect around her weary face.

"Am I dead?"

At first the question didn't register. It seemed far away in a fog. Then it repeated itself.

"Am I dead? I must be. You must be an angel. You're too pretty to be a demon and they don't have halos." It was a hoarse croak. Then there was a groan. Madeline's eyes opened wide.

"What? Huh? Are you…" But her patient's eyes fluttered shut again. "Doc! Doc Becker!" she hollered.

The medical practitioner strolled into the room. "Well, what is it? Did he finally die so I can get my operating room back?" he growled.

"Doc Becker! Really?" Her tone was scolding. "He is not dead. I think he was just awake."

"Let me check him, child. Doggone womenfolk and their wishful thinking. Probably figures he proposed or called her an angel or something like that. If 'n he was fifty and fat, she'd of probably left him to die like he shoulda done days ago." The doctor continued to mutter as he checked the unconscious man. "Well, missy, his breathing seems strong and his fever is gone. His heart's still beating. That bullet must have missed everything important. If he wakes up, he's got a chance. Get some food into him if he does. Notice I said *if*, not *when*."

"I will make sure he is fed when he wakes up. And he is not fifty and fat, so that is irrelevant." Madeline blushed. Come to think of it, he was kind of good-looking.

"Harrumph," the doctor snorted. "Irrelevant my foot. I'll make sure there's some strong beef broth on the stove in the office keeping warm. Maybe he'll get a chance to eat some of it before he dies."

"Honestly, Doctor Becker, with your optimistic outlook, it is a wonder any of your patients live."

"All of them die eventually, but that's got nothing to do with my doctoring. That's just a fact of life." He chuckled softly.

Even the excitement of Jim waking momentarily could not keep Madeline's eyes from closing, and she dozed in the warm sun. When she awoke, she noticed Jim's eyes were looking blearily at her.

"You're awake," she exclaimed. "You must be hungry and thirsty."

Jim just stared dumbly at her as she brought a cup of water to him. "Just a little to start with. Too much at once isn't good for you." She held his head up and tipped the cup carefully to his lips. Next was the beef broth, which he took gratefully.

"Thank you," he managed to say as she wiped some broth from his chin. "I thought I was dead. I even saw an angel, I think, but they didn't answer when I talked to them."

"It was not an angel you were talking to earlier. You spoke to me, but I think you were delirious. I am surely not an angel."

"Who are you?" Exhaustion overtook Jim and he drifted back into unconsciousness before she could respond.

Through the next few days Jim drifted between wakefulness, when Madeline fed him as much broth and soup as he could manage, and fitful sleep. Nightmares plagued his sleep. Visions of those who killed his family and the ghostly face of Taggert haunted his dreams, but his strength was returning and the nightmares subsided.

"Well, young feller, I guess you can't," quipped the doctor when Jim was finally able to move.

"Can't what, Doc?"

"Well, when that there young lady dragged your all-but-dead carcass in here and told me 'he just can't die,' I guess you've proved her right over all my predictions to the contrary."

"Thanks, Doc." Jim grinned.

"Don't thank me. You thank that stubborn little girl over there." He pointed to Madeline who was bringing Jim a meal of solid food. "I was ready to call the undertaker, but she wouldn't hear of it. She sat by you and fussed and nursed you through more than you have a right to have lived through."

"Thank you, Madeline," Jim said. They had exchanged names when Jim was finally able to talk, but until now he had not realized it was her that had insisted on his care. "Maybe I was right when I thought I saw an angel." He smiled.

Blushing deeply, she handed him his food. "You eat and quit flirting," she ordered, then blushed, and left the room pleased by his comment.

"She's a good girl and deserves a good man, not a man hunter. Your scars could mean a lot of things, but them there outlaws saying it was personal leaves a man to wonder." Doc Becker left it at that. "Speaking of wonders, it's a wonder that bullet went through where it did without hitting something important."

Now that he could sit up and take nourishment, Jim's strength grew day by day. It wasn't long before he was able to hobble around town. He was growing restless to be on the trail, but his horses and money had been taken by Jacobs. They had left his pistols and holsters. He could sell them for money, but Jim would not part with them. He needed them to continue his hunt, and he still had a bit of recovering to do.

Sixteen

hile Jim was still unconscious, the posse had returned having lost the trail of the outlaws. The gang had scattered with the intention of re-gathering at a predetermined location many miles away. Things had grown too hot for the Jacobs gang in Northern Wyoming territory. Maybe Idaho would be the place to hole up for a while. Even though the posse did not catch up with any living gang members, the lazy circling of vultures led them to another grisly discovery.

Nobody had bothered to bury Taggert. Coyotes had discovered his body during the night and the vultures were squabbling over the bloated remains when the sheriff's posse drove them off. The damaged arm and hip were not readily apparent, but the cause of death was. The rope burns still showed clearly around the throat of the dead man. A quick search of the dead man revealed nothing. His friends had stripped his body of anything of value or that would help identify him.

The posse rolled the dead man into a nearby wash and covered the body. That job accomplished, they set out for town. The hunt was over for them. It would be fruitless. Besides, they had wives and families waiting for them back home.

Three weeks after the abortive attempt to capture the robbers, the marshal walked into Doc Becker's."How's the patient, Doc?"

"He's off gallivanting around town with Miss Stark right now, why? Is something wrong?"

"No. Just wondering if he'd seen anyone else out there. You know we found a man who had been hanged a little ways from where the stage was held up didn't you?"

"I'd heard rumors, but rumors are rumors. What makes you think young Jim might know anything?"

"Nothing really. Just thought I'd ask him. You take care, Doc."

The doctor scowled thoughtfully after the marshal.

The sun was setting over the mountains. The crimson sky kissed the shoulders of the purple range. Snowy peaks turned red looking like the jagged teeth of some gigantic prehistoric beast. Then the light softened, turning to softer pastels instead of the deep red. A cool breeze blew down from the craggy peaks, and Madeline instinctively moved closer to Jim for warmth. "They're beautiful," she breathed.

"Beautiful and deadly," Jim said quietly. "Too many places for criminals to hide and too many ways for a man to die up there." His melancholy statement brought a sideways glance from the girl by his side.

"Why such a morbid comment, James? That seems such an odd thing to say about something so pretty." She stepped back to look at him as she spoke.

"Because it's the truth." He seemed lost in thought as he stared at the horizon. Then he looked at her expression and continued, "It is beautiful to look at, though. Come on. You have about worn me out with all this walking around, but it seems to be helping."

"Tomorrow I need to find some way to get an outfit. I've been laid up too long already and need to be up and useful. Besides," he said, touching his latest bullet scar, "I still have some business to attend to."

"James," Madeline exclaimed. "Don't even think of such things. That is revenge. Besides, the marshal lost their trail weeks ago. That, and you are in no condition for anything like that." Her face was red and her hazel eyes blazed with emotions. "I will not listen to such talk!"

"I had better get you home." Jim's voice was despondent. He did not like that he had made Madeline upset, but he couldn't run his life based on a woman's feelings. How could she understand?

Leaving her at her home, he thought as the moonlight touched her hair it did give a radiance much like the angel he mistook her for when he first saw her. She was very pretty even when upset.

Jim returned to Doc Becker's. "Doc, what do I owe you for all you've done? It's about time for me to get out of your hair."

The doctor muttered a bit then gave Jim a figure. "Don't fret none too much. Pay me when you can. Madeline has been a help around here, and I don't reckon she would have hung around and helped out without you being here.

"The marshal stopped by while you were out. Mentioned that dead man they found. Said he'd been hanged. Probably never know how it happened or who done it."

"Probably not. I'll be moving out tomorrow. I got hold of Wells Fargo and they are moving some money for me. I have to get me an outfit, so I'll be around for a little longer. That Madeline is a fine girl."

The doctor's eyes were hard. "That she is," he said with a clipped voice, "but not for a man hunter. She don't suspect nothing, but I got an idea you know a bit more about these stage robbers than you're letting on. Not that I think you were involved, but they know you, and I think you know them. She's a good girl. She deserves someone who ain't on the edge."

"The edge?" Jim's voice was incredulous.

"Don't get me wrong. I ain't saying you're a bad sort, but I can see it in your eyes. And, your knife is Cheyenne. If you aren't careful, you will kill the wrong man. You've something eating at you. Her pa hasn't said nothing because he dotes on that girl, and she sees nothing but good in everybody. Again, not saying you're a bad sort, but just not her sort."

"Thanks, Doc." The doctor's words were painful because they were closer to the truth than Jim wanted to admit. "I'll be out of here in the morning after we settle up. Then, what I do won't be your concern anymore. As for the knife, it's a good blade." Jim walked into the parlor where he had been sleeping since able to walk. Even though he was recovering well, he still tired quickly. He was asleep as soon as he lay down.

The next morning Jim visited the Wells Fargo office and picked up the money he had transferred to the local office. He paid the doctor what was owed and visited the local livery to see what kind of stock they had to offer. He wanted not only a good saddle horse but also a pack mule. Plenty of men wouldn't take a mule even as a pack animal. Jim knew their value and preferred them to a packhorse.

None of the saddle stock was what he sought, but a big mule with watchful eyes caught his attention. The mule was ugly and tried to step on Jim's foot as he walked around him, but he looked strong and took the carrot Jim offered him gently enough. Jim looked at several other animals before asking about the mule. The upshot was he got the mule, a second-hand saddle, bridle, rifle scabbard, and saddlebags for the price the hostler wanted for one horse. A cowhand would scoff at a mule, but a good mule would go all day and all night, just not very fast. As a pack animal, a mule could not be beat.

Jim had made the acquaintance of a few of the ranchers during his short forays about town. One raised some Morgans mixed with good mustang stock. Saddling the mule, Jim rode in the direction of the M/M Ranch. If he could get a good deal on one of those Morgan crosses, he figured he would have a good trail horse.

On his way out of town he ignored the jeers of the local cowpunchers. Most of them would rather walk than ride a mule, but Jim rode with his head up and the mule pranced as though on parade. He pranced, as much as a mule can prance. Suddenly a friendly voice reached his ears. "Oh, Jim, I'm so glad you picked Wally. They were going to shoot him instead of continuing to feed him. They said he was too ugly for anyone to buy. I think he's handsome."

Jim halted the mule, and Madeline stepped from the boardwalk of the general store to rub the complacent mule's nose. He gently snuffled her hand looking for the lump of sugar she always had for him. "And he is very spirited."

"Handsome? I might call him sturdy, but if you ask me, he's ugly as a post."

Wally rolled his eyes as if he understood his new owner's words. "Don't say that, Jim! He is not ugly, and you will hurt his feelings talking like that."

"Well, right now he needs to be feeling his hooves moving us to the M/M. There I hope to get a good saddle horse and then we will be back to town for supplies. I've also heard there is a dance this Saturday if you have no plans."

He chuckled. "Wally would like it if you attended with me. We shall return."

He gently turned the mule away from Madeline and rode in the direction of the ranch. He didn't have a big stake, but he should have enough for at least one good mount and some supplies.

Seventeen

J im was still weak, but it felt good to be back in the saddle, even if it was astride a mule . Wally gave Jim no problems until they reached the edge of a creek they needed to ford. The mule suddenly balked, and no matter how Jim urged him, he would not move any closer to the water's edge.

His long ears laid back and his fore feet braced, the mule brayed his displeasure. Jim thought he had discovered the reason he got the mule so cheaply. Wally backed a few steps from the water and his eyes rolled with fear.

"Come on you stubborn half-wit mule! It's just water! What is wrong with you?" Jim kicked the stubborn beast in the ribs, but the mule still balked.

Without warning, a tawny shape appeared in the middle of the trail on the opposite bank. The young tom cougar stared at the man and the mule and snarled. Whether by scent or hearing, Wally had sensed the danger. Much like Balaam's donkey, which had sensed the angel, Wally balked and kept his rider safe.

Drawing the Winchester from the scabbard, Jim was prepared if the cougar attacked but did not fire. He had no idea what the mule's reaction would be to gunfire and thought now was not the time to find out. Instead Jim shouted and waved his hat in the air startling the big cat. It snarled viciously once, then fled into the brush along the creek.

After a few minutes, Wally placidly advanced across the shallow stream and continued on his way. "You may be ugly as a post, but you sure aren't as dumb as one." Jim patted the mule's neck and the chestnut-colored animal perked his ears up as if pleased by the compliment.

A short time later they plodded into the ranch yard of the M/M. The owner, Dave Nivel, strolled up to them. The wrangler and a couple of riders were working the kinks out of a few half-broken horses in one of the corrals. Dust boiled over the scene as horse and rider dueled to see who would master whom. Generally the job was all but complete before the rider ever got into the saddle, but a good horse still liked to make sure their rider knew they still had plenty of spirit.

"So Swanson finally got rid of that brute, huh? I figured that mule was destined to be coyote bait. What possessed you to ride that thing out here?"

"Mr. Nivel, Wally here is a fine mule," he said, patting Wally's back. "As a matter of fact, saved my bacon back a couple miles. If he hadn't balked when he sensed that lion, him or I, or both of us would have been in a bad fix. He stopped cold and would not go a step closer, but he never panicked or bucked. As soon as the cat was gone, he strolled along like nothing was ever wrong.

"As far as riding him goes, they did not have any saddle stock at the livery to my liking, so I saddled up Wally and came out here. It was that or walk. I prefer riding.

"Hey, just curious, why M/M? It isn't your initials or anything."

David laughed. "It was kind of a joke at first. We were working to improve the mustangs and brought in the Morgans so M/M. Anybody riding one of our horses knows where it came from and what it is."

"Well, I would sure admire to ride one of your horses, if they can be had for what I can pay. A good trail horse with plenty of stamina. Speed is nice, but I'm looking for a stayer."

"I might have a few that would fit your needs. Why don't you swing down from that old crow bait and have some coffee. Then we can talk horses. "

Wally gave Nivel the evil eye as if he knew he had been insulted. His left ear flopped over like it had gone limp. Jim swung from the saddle tying Wally to the hitching rail. "Miss Stark thinks this old mule is handsome," Jim laughed. "I think he's as ugly as a stump, but he showed himself pretty smart and steady today at that creek. Let's have some of that coffee and take a look at those horses you've got."

After coffee and some discussion of local politics, of which Jim had very little knowledge or interest, Dave Nivel led the way to one of the multiple corrals. Climbing to the top rail, Jim watched the horses as they moved around the enclosures. All were excellent horseflesh, and choosing one from the bunch was tough. A tall sorrel had his attention until a dapple gray pushed through the herd.

While about a hand shorter than the sorrel, the gray moved well and showed more fire than the other mounts. He held his head high and his eyes missed nothing. His ears twisted as if constantly alert for sounds that might mean danger. Jim believed, like many a western man, that a horse without some spirit would let you down when you most needed them. The dappled gray had spirit and an eye that promised mischief to an unwary or inexperienced rider. Well-muscled, the horse looked sound.

"What about that dapple gray gelding? He doesn't look too bad."

"Doesn't look too bad you say? That's a heck of a bit of horseflesh, but he has a dislike for greenhorns. He's a trail horse, not a town horse."

"That's what I figured and what I need. What would it take for you to part with him? And remember, I already spent a fortune on that prize mule." Jim chuckled.

For a while the men dickered as Jim checked the horse more closely. The more he looked the more satisfied he was with his choice and a price was arrived at. A loop was dabbed over the gray's head and he was led out to stand beside Wally.

The mule gave the gelding a disapproving look as saddle and bridle were swapped from his back to the dapple gray. Jim spoke gently to the horse during the process, stroking his sleek neck and strong shoulder. He swung astride, and almost before he was settled, the gelding decided to make sure his new rider deserved to be in the saddle.

Jim was ready but far from fully recovered. Gritting his teeth and holding tight, Jim pulled the horse's head up to control the pitching. He succeeded in keeping the spirited half-ton of hurricane from taking the bit in his teeth and really setting to. Even so, it was all Jim could do to stay astride as the horse swapped ends twice and pitched like a rowboat on a rough sea. After a fine display of bucking, the dapple gray decided Jim was worthy to stay in the saddle and settled down.

Jim's face was ashen, and he hoped he had not ripped his wound open again. "You are right. This is a hunk of horse-flesh. I just hope he doesn't decide to see who's boss quite that way every time I mount up."

Jim rode back to town with Wally in tow. He had sufficient left in his poke to put together enough of an outfit to last a couple weeks. If he did not find the trail in that time, he would be forced to return to the Lazy H until he found a fresh place to resume his search. He was impatient to find those responsible for the death of his family, but a few more days to recover were needed. Besides, he had asked Madeline to the dance on Saturday.

Saturday evening arrived, and Jim had regained much of his strength. The dapple gray had settled in his mind that Jim belonged in the saddle, so the morning disputes had settled to a few crow hops just to make sure Jim was ready for the day. Rugged living and hard work had made his body recover quickly once he started healing.

The music had already begun when Jim arrived with Madeline on his arm. The blue dress she wore was pulled tight at her narrow waist and accentuated the curves of her slender young body. The flush of excitement brought color to her cheeks. Dark curls were held neatly back from her face by dainty yellow ribbons. More than one man looked when she walked in. She chattered excitedly to Jim and her parents and was oblivious to the attention she received.

She dragged Jim onto the dance floor as the next song started. Her cheerful exuberance transferred itself to her dancing as Jim twirled her about the floor. Her laughter and stream of cheerful banter seemed to overshadow the musicians with its own musical lilt. Jim hardly realized when the fiddlers stopped.

As the band stopped, Madeline took Jim's hand and led him to a group of other young ladies, quickly introducing him to friends and acquaintances.

"So this is what has been occupying your time of late," remarked a young woman introduced as Marie Baxter. She was an attractive blond, but her brown eyes were hard and calculating. Unlike Madeline, whose natural beauty came not only from her outward appearance but was something that flowed from within her, Marie's beauty went no deeper than her skin. While Madeline never realized she was attractive and did not think of herself as such, Marie knew it, flaunted it, and used it to her advantage. She did not yet realize that the outer beauty fades but the inner beauty shines through for a lifetime.

"Jim is not a what. He is a who," Madeline responded. "And yes, he has been keeping me busy since I returned from Ohio. I have been helping Doctor Becker tend to him, and now he is almost fully recovered. "

"Oh, I'll bet you have been tending him," was the snide reply.

Before Madeline could reply, Jim interceded. "Yes, she has been very helpful. When others, including the good doctor, were ready to fit me for a pine box, she refused to accept it. She fed me when I was too weak to feed myself, and when I wanted to skip the exercise the doctor told me to do, she would not let me.

"She was indeed a help and always a lady. To imply anything else would be an insult. If a man had implied such, I would be forced to shoot him." A waltz started. "Madeline, I'm a bit out of practice, but shall we?" Jim led her to the dance floor.

They left Marie red-faced and glowering as they glided away together. She was unused to being thwarted or having any man speak to her in such a way. He would not get away with it, she thought. Then a dashing young cowboy led her to the dance floor and she forgot all about it.

Madeline giggled. "I don't think anyone has ever shot Marie down like that before. Thank you, sir, for defending my honor." She laughed again as they moved with the music.

The night seemed to fly by and Jim danced with several of the young ladies and some of the not-quite-so-young ladies as well. Before he realized it, he was walking Madeline home. She held tightly to his arm.

They lingered on the front porch as he looked into her warm hazel eyes. There was invitation and promise in those eyes. The invitation to call her his own, the promise of love and forever. Her eyes shined as she stood on tiptoe and kissed him shyly. She blushed. "I'm sorry. You must think me brazen."

"No," he replied quietly. "I would never think you brazen, impulsive perhaps, but definitely not brazen. You are a lady and quite possibly the angel I took you for when first I saw you."

Even in the soft light of the moon he could see the color creep in to her cheeks. "Don't say such things, James. Not unless you mean them," she whispered, keeping her eyes down.

"Do you think me one who would bear false witness? I am only telling you the truth." He took her chin and gently turned her face toward his. As he brought his face toward her, he felt a slight twinge where the bullet had been removed from his body. He gave a slight grimace.

"Jim, are you okay? Are you hurt?"

"No. No, just a bit sore. I think I overdid it tonight. Just a reminder of what I have to do."

"James, please don't speak of such things. You know how I feel about it. I couldn't stand the thought of something happening to you. After all Doctor Becker did, you are just going to go out and get shot again. I can't stand to think of that."

"Then I guess you had best think of something else. They owe a debt, and I intend to make them pay it. Scripture says, 'Eye for eye, tooth for tooth, life for life.' I'll be leaving tomorrow."

Tears streamed down her face as he turned to leave. She fled into the house with sobs wracking her frame. He could be such a good man. Why was he so filled with hate? Then she remembered the scars she had seen on his body while she had helped Doc Becker treat his wound. "Scripture also says to forgive," she whispered.

"He's leaving?" She had not heard her father enter her room. "I'm sorry, sweetheart." What else could he say? To say, "I warned you," would only serve to make her feel foolish and hurt her even more.

"He is going after the men who shot him, but I think there is more to it than that." Her father sat beside her on the bed. "He never spoke of his family much, but he said they were gone. This was not the first time he had been shot, Daddy. He has some awful scars. I saw them while Doctor Becker was patching him up. I thought..." Her voice trailed off and she wept softly for a moment.

"I know, Maddie, I know, but sometimes a wild one just won't allow himself to be tamed." Her father had not called her Maddie since she was a little girl in need of comfort. He put his big arms around her shoulders.

"Do you think he will come back?"

"No," he replied softly after a moment's thought. He shook his head slowly. "He won't be back. I am very sorry. I think your injured puppy is more wolf than dog, and he isn't ready to be tamed."

"Oh, Daddy." She put her head on his shoulder and cried as her mother looked in from the doorway.

The next morning Jim headed out before dawn. He planned to make use of the coolness of the morning for traveling. Before leaving town, though, he rode to a small meadow where he remembered some wild flowers growing and plucked some of the brightest ones. These he left along with a note on the Stark's doorstep. Madeline's mother found them when she opened the door to sweep the porch.

> Dear Madeline,
>
> Please forgive me for any pain I have caused you. I believe you are indeed an angel of light in a dark world. Thank you for your kindness.

It was signed simply, James.

Eighteen

There had been no stage holdups since Jim had been shot, so the place for him to start was where the holdup took place.

If he found nothing, he would return to their last camp and try to pick up some sign of them there. He doubted that they had returned to that camp, but he would give it a try.

Two weeks of searching netted no results. Jacobs and his gang had simply pulled up stakes and vanished. He was out of coffee and had eaten the last of his beans the day before. It was time to leave the trail for now. He would keep his ears and eyes open for any word of the killers, but for now he was stuck. He brushed out the signs of his camp and swung astride the gray, pointing the gelding toward the Lazy H. He would have to live off the land a few days.

It was late in the afternoon several days later when Jim rode into the ranch yard. He stripped the saddle from the gray and the pack from Wally. He rubbed both animals down and forked them some hay before turning them loose in the corral. Tom met him as he was coming out of the barn where he stowed his gear.

"Saw you ride in. A little different outfit than you rode out with, but from the look of that dapple, you didn't trade down much."

"He's a good trail horse. Wally there" — he indicated the mule — "I'm not so sure if I traded up, down, or sideways on him, but he's a steady mule."

Tom laughed. Then his face turned serious. "We heard you'd been shot. They said one of the bandits said it was personal. They almost killed you again, Jim, why don't you leave it before they do?"

Jim stared hard at Tom. His eyes burned like blue flames. "There are worse things than being dead," he growled. "Like no justice for those who deserve justice."

Before Tom could respond, Sarah came racing around the corner of the barn and turned to look behind her. Her face was flushed with childish joy, and a few seconds later a butter-ball of a puppy scampered around the corner chasing her. She squealed with delight as the puppy barked and growled in mock fierceness.

"You can't catch me. You can't catch me," she giggled. She turned to run on in her game of chase and crashed head-long into Tom.

Her father scooped her up and tossed her into the air catching her lightly. He lifted the laughing youngster over his head. "He might not be able to catch you, but Daddy sure can." She was dangling upside down in her father's grasp when she noticed Jim. "Daddy, look, Jim is back!" She pointed.

"I saw, sweetheart. We were just talking." Tom put his daughter gently back on the ground and tussled her hair. "He just got back."

The puppy was bouncing around Sarah's feet and tugging playfully at the edge of her dress. She wrapped her arms around the squirming bundle of fur and lifted him from the ground so Jim could see him. He was covered with yellow-and-brown fur and had floppy ears. The puppy barked and wiggled, but Sarah held him tight. "Rufus, this is Jim. He's a friend of ours."

Jim let the puppy sniff his hand and then scratched between those floppy ears. "He is sure a cute pup."

"The Galloways gived him."

"Gave him, not gived him, Sarah," her father corrected.

"The Galloways gave him to me. He is so smart. He gots, I mean he has one blue eye and one brown eye. See?" She turned the puppy's face toward Jim so he could see, and he sure enough did have one blue eye and one brown. He had heard of such eye colors in some of the herding dogs but had never seen it.

"Well, I'll be. That makes him a very special pup then. It surely does."

The days turned to weeks, the weeks to months and the months toward another year. Jim worked hard at the ranch and developed the gold claim, but each time he heard some report of Jacobs or the possibility of a sighting, he would saddle up and ride. The relationship with the Daltons grew strained. What may have grown into a strong friendship was nothing more than a business arrangement. It was profitable for all, but most of the work fell on Tom since Jim was constantly riding off to check out some rumor. Each time he would return more obsessed with his quest for vengeance.

Five times he had ridden out before the snows closed in the ranch. The snow in this part of Montana made travel almost impossible, so Jim waited impatiently for the spring thaw, even though travel was nearly stopped, the ranch work only increased. Water holes needed to be kept open for stock.

Trails to sheltered valleys and haystacks needed to be kept open as well. The occasional foolish cow, steer, or bull needed to be pulled from the drifts they had floundered into.

"Jim," Dinah called. "Tom killed a big old tom turkey and I'm making dried apple pie and cranberry dressing. The hands are joining us for dinner and we would like you to join us as well."

"It sounds really good but—"

She cut him off. "It's Christmas, and you shouldn't be eating alone. Tom took Sarah and Rufus to get a tree, and little Thomas even knows something is going on today. I've been cooking up a big feast and don't want my efforts to go to waste."

"Christmas? I lost track of time. I couldn't intrude on your family, and besides, I've no gifts for any of you."

"Fiddlesticks! You would not be intruding. How could you even think that? As for gifts, you gave us part of this ranch. What else could you give us? Besides, we are celebrating the birth of Christ, not looking for presents. Dinner starts at four today and goes until everyone is too stuffed to move.

"You've been spending too much time working alone or working that claim. You need a rest. It's not good for a man to be alone as much as you are. You're growing as hard as those mountains with all you running after bandits and work-ing alone." She had mentioned his obsession with the Jacobs gang more than once before.

"All right, I'll be there for dinner, just no talk about me *not* hunting those that killed my family." His tone was gruff but resigned.

"Fair enough, four o'clock. We'll be looking for you."

Dinah had been cooking up a storm. Along with the turkey and cranberry dressing were mounds of potatoes with gravy, fresh baked biscuits, corn, squash, and of course apple pie topped with fresh whipped cream. Venison and roasted quail were added to the feast. As promised, everyone had more than enough to eat.

The tree had been erected and handmade decorations adorned its limbs and gifts were scattered beneath it. After Tom read the story of the birth of Christ from the book of Luke, he began to hand out gifts with Sarah acting as daddy's little helper. There were gifts for Little Tom, Sarah, and the hands. Watching the warmth and love shown between all these present made Jim feel like an outsider. They had each other. The loss of his family had left him hollow inside, and he filled that hollow with his desire for revenge.

Jim rose to his feet. "I'd best head out to the bunkhouse." He started for the door. "Wait, Jim," cried Sarah. "You haven't opened your gift yet. Daddy picked it out, but I helped wrap it, and Mommy made part of it too. I helped sew the buttons on it. Oops." She placed her hand over her mouth and turned away quickly. "I'm sorry. I almost gave it away. Here, you can open it now." She plunked a large box in Jim's hands before he could protest.

"But, I don't have anything for you. I can't accept this." He stood uncertainly and looked around the room. He started to hand the package back.

"You gave us a house, silly," countered Sarah. "Daddy and Mommy and me and Little Tommy gots a place to stay. You gave it to us, didn't you?" Who could argue with the logic of such an earnest little girl?

"You win," he conceded with a smile. Reseating himself on the stool he had been occupying while others opened their gifts of shirts and belts or the children's toys and teddy bears, Jim carefully began to open his gift.

Sarah watched expectantly as she had when the others had opened their gifts. She bounced up and down and clapped her hands. "Hurry up! Hurry up!" She almost shouted.

At her instigation, he smiled and opened the package. Inside he found a hand tooled leather sheath that looked to be a perfect fit for the Cheyenne knife he carried. Affixed to the sheath was a pouch containing a good Arkansas whetstone. The shirt on top of which they were laid was a soft wool. Dark blue in color, it had hand-stitched patterns on each of the breast pockets.

"I had to guess at the size, so I hope it fits. It should help keep you warm though, and Sarah did help with the buttons on everybody's shirts."

"I don't know what to say," Jim muttered softly. "Thanks. Thank you very much."

"You're very welcome." Tom smiled. "I noticed your sheath was getting a bit worn, and I figured you could use a new one and a good stone. Sarah helped me pick it out. If there's any chew marks on it, that was little Tom giving his approval." The hands had received similar gifts of shirts and pocketknives or tobacco pouches.

"Well, Sarah," asked Bob, one of the hands, as he patted his overstuffed belly, "didn't Santer Claus bring you nothing? You been handing out gifts, but I ain't seen you open none."

"You mean Santa Clause? Nope, he didn't bring me any gifts. Mommy and Daddy did. You know that."

"Santa didn't bring you nothing? Are you sure? Cause I found something out in the bunkhouse with your name on it. Windy and me found it, and I'm sure it's from Santa." Bob pulled a package from where he had hidden it in his coat pocket. "See, it says right here, 'Sarah,' and I think S.C. is Santa Clause, ain't it?" He pointed to the tag.

"Do you know who Santa Claus is for real?" asked Sarah. When she began to tell the story of Saint Nicholas, Jim slipped out the door and stood on the front porch watching the storm clouds building off to the northwest. As the clouds thickened, the few stars that had been visible in the early evening sky were blotted out by the strengthening storm. The darkness was shutting out the lights one by one, much like revenge was crowding out the light in his heart. The difference was he could see the clouds amassing in the sky, but he was blind to his own black storm.

"Hello, the house!" The call came from someone on the edge of the light. Jim had noticed the stranger's approach. The rider kept his hands in view and, following Western etiquette, had called out without dismounting.

"Ride on up," Jim invited. As he was speaking, Tom opened the door and stepped onto the porch. "C'mon in," Tom said. "It's Christmas, and we can't be like the innkeeper and turn folks away. There's plenty to eat if you're hungry. You can put your horse in the lean-to with the others and then come in and sit."

"Thanks. I've ridden a piece and sure wouldn't mind some vittles." His drawl was thick. He turned his horse toward the indicated shelter. Tom turned back inside, and Jim watched the stranger while he stripped the gear from his horse and stowed it. Then he fed the animal some hay and a scoop of oats. While rubbing the steel-dust gelding down with a handful of straw, he checked it over closely to ensure it was suffering no ill effects from its travel. Only after the horse was cared for did the man head toward the house to meet his own need for food and warmth.

"Some place a feller can wash up? I hate to intrude on folks without at least washing up a mite."

"There's a wash basin just inside the door. Mrs. Dalton keeps it full most of the time. She sets a good table too," Jim responded.

"Don't see a lot of travelers this time of year. The passes to the northwest are likely snowed in for the year." Jim said it as a simple statement with no question implied.

"That could be why I ain't seen too many folks." The stranger laughed. "They got better sense than to be out in the snow with a storm coming on. Trouble is, I don't always show good sense, 'specially when hunting two-legged wolves. Lost 'em when the snow wiped out their trail down in Wyoming. Trying to get back home now without freezing."

"Let's get out of the cold. You must be ready to warm up by now." Jim led the way into the house. He liked that the man took such good care of his mount, but he had questions. Why would a man be traveling in this weather, and who were the "two-legged wolves?"

As soon as the man washed up, Dinah handed him a cup of hot cider laced with just a touch of "Christmas cheer" to warm the traveler's bones. He sipped gratefully and held the warm mug with both hands to warm his fingers. "Thank you, ma'am. That sure is what a body needs after a ride on a cold night like this."

"You are most welcome, Mr. ...., I'm sorry. Where are our manners? I'm Dinah, and this is my husband, Tom." She continued the introductions. "And what should we call you?"

"You can call me warmer than I was outside, but that would be a long handle. Most folks just call me Max. Short for Maxwell Bartholomew Vanderbilt, at your service. That's why most folks just call me Max. To say the whole thing is a mouthful."

"Well, Max, we were about to have some more pie, but there is plenty of food if you are hungry, and I suspect you are. Please help yourself and I will make sure that there is some pie saved for you. You can hang your hat and coat on the pegs by the door." Dinah pointed to the rack on the wall.

"Thank you kindly, ma'am. I'm obliged. As for being hungry, my belly button is on intimate terms with my back-bone about now." Max sat his now-empty cup down, shrugged out of his buffalo coat, and hung it and his hat on the pegs. The bulky coat had camouflaged his lean, almost skinny frame. Strapped around his thin waist was a gun belt with the holster on his left hip, butt forward, for a cross draw. The old Dragoon Colt looked almost too large for his small frame, but he wore it with the ease of one born to it.

"I hate to intrude on folks," he said retrieving his coffee mug, "it being Christmas and all, but I didn't cotton to the idea of sleeping in a snow cave when I might be able to find a hayloft instead."

"It's no imposition," Tom stated. "As for the hayloft, we've a couple spare bunks in the bunkhouse and that should be warmer than the barn. More comfortable too I would imagine."

Dinah gave Max a plate heaped with food. He dug in hungrily. "Sure is better than beans and salt pork." He managed to comment around a mouth full of food.

Sarah had finished her narration on Santa Claus with the legend of Saint Nicholas leaving gold coins in the stock-ings of three young girls in desperate need of a dowry so they wouldn't be sold as slaves. (The real story of Saint Nicholas) She noticed Max. "You're not s'posed to talk with food in your mouth." She had been admonished numerous times herself regarding such behavior.

"Sarah!" her mother spoke quickly. "Max is our guest and that is no way to treat a guest. You apologize." Dinah's stern brown eyes were on her daughter.

"I'm sorry, sir," Sarah said with downcast eyes.

"Well, youngster, don't think nothing of it. I get out on the trail sometimes and plumb forget my manners. You was right as rain. It ain't proper manners for a man to talk with his mouth full. The food was just so good I forgot myself. Now if you could help me in the manners department, is it polite to ask for a second helping when your plate gets empty?"

Sarah smiled and twirled herself back and forth looking shyly at the thin man before her. She stopped and thought for a second. Biting her lower lip she glanced thoughtfully at the ceiling. "Yes," she said after the pause, "But you have to say please." Then, in a conspiratorial whisper, she added, "but save some room for pie. Mommy makes the bestest pie in the whole wide world."

"I'll do just that." Max winked at Sarah.

"When you empty your plate, Max, just go ahead and reload it. Like Sarah said, though, save room for some pie. My beautiful bride does make the best I've ever had." Tom smiled at Dinah who beamed.

"So is that why you married me, Mister Thomas Dalton? Because of my apple pie?"

Tom winked at her and smiled. "There might be a few other reasons," he said playfully. A silly grin plastered on his face.

Her face turned crimson and she swatted him on the shoulder. "You should be ashamed of yourself," she snapped. But she smiled as she turned to the bench where the pies sat, secretly pleased that her husband still noticed her and made her feel like a woman. He had a glimpse of the smile before she turned away. She still made his pulse race like no other woman could. He knew he was one very lucky man.

After pie and another few cups of coffee or warm cider, the children were tucked in and good nights were said. The men trudged through the blowing snow to the bunkhouse. During the last hour, as they had talked, the storm had started and it was a true Montana blizzard. A gale force wind was howling off the craggy ridges. Trees bent and whipped about and a few lost their grip on the earth and toppled over. The huge flakes of snow fell nearly horizontally, almost hiding the bunkhouse only a few dozen yards away. Tree limbs already heavy with snow were torn from the trunks by the burden of new snow and the wind.

The wind sneaking in through the open door of the building blew out two of the three lamps and threatened to extinguish the third before the door was forced closed against it. The storm raged through the night and the next two days and nights. The men took turns feeding the stock that was moved from the lean-to, into the barn. Nobody dared venture further than to the barn and to the house for food.

"Sure am glad I turned in when I saw you folks' lights. I don't know as I'd have ever gotten home if I'd have been caught outdoors in this." It was the second night of the blizzard, and along with the snow, the temperatures had been falling steadily. "I'd hate to think of any good man caught in something like this," Jim responded. "There are a few, though, that wouldn't worry me if they found themselves out there." Jim was in a black mood being cooped up. "You said something about hunting two-legged wolves when you rode in. Are you a lawman?" Jim asked.

Max was somewhat slow to respond. "Of sorts you might say. I'm unofficial."

"A bounty hunter?" sneered Kenny. Disgust was thick in his voice.

"Nope, not that neither. Hired by a couple of mining and transportation concerns to keep their passengers and interests safe. Was doing pretty well until this last holdup. Eight, nine men stopped the stage. Killed the shotgun guard out of hand. The poor kid didn't even have a gun in his hands when they shot him down. Guess they didn't like him trying to stop one of them from rough-handling a lady. They let the lady be after that, though, but took the holiday payroll for a couple of the mines. Neither the miners nor the owners was happy about that. They'll be even less happy when I get back."

"Not many gangs use that many to stop a stage, do they?" Jim already knew the answer but wanted confirmation.

"Nope, only about two or three of them. There's Pullens, Jacobs, maybe Sandoval. That's about it that I know of."

Jim gleaned more information over the next couple days. While the storm roared down from the mountains, the men talked, repaired ropes, and played cards for matchsticks. The storm broke three days after Christmas ushering in bitter cold.

"I sure do appreciate you folks taking me in, but I've got to be going. I've got to report in. That won't be pleasant, but there's no sense putting it off. So long and thanks again!" Given extra food for the trail, Max bundled into his buffalo coat and headed northeast riding his big steel dust gelding.

Nineteen

The men saddled up and were getting ready to ride out and check stock. They led a pair of large, shaggy draft horses with hair hanging down over their hooves. The huge animals would be used to pull downed trees off of the trails and in some cases to pull a drag to clear snow. The pair seemed imperious to cold and weighed more than twice what the cow ponies did. The quickness and speed of a cow pony was not needed where these brutes would be used. The men carried axes and shovels on their saddles.

When Jim led Wally out, the mule brayed loudly in protest. "Come on you flop-eared old jughead," Jim growled at the balking mule. "We don't have all day."

"We got the Clydesdales, Jim, we don't need Wally. Leave him to get fat and lazy. We'll work him enough come spring." Tom was ready to get to work.

"You might not need him, Tom, but I will. I'm going after those holdup men Max was trailing. The trail's getting colder while Wally is braying about the weather."

"You're riding off on a cold trail while we have enough work for ten men after that storm? You expect us to do all the work while you're off chasing shadows? You don't even know if it was Jacobs or not!" Tom was incredulous.

"Look, Tom," Jim snapped. "I gave you working partnership in this ranch with the stipulation that I can ride when I decide to. If you have more work than you can handle, you figure it out. I'm going after that gang!" Jim's voice was surly.

Sarah had come out all bundled for the cold to play with Rufus. The little girl had witnessed the exchange and saw Wally rolling his eyes against the cold.

"You can't talk to Daddy like that!" She shouted through the thick scarf wrapped around her face. "And Wally doesn't like the cold. You leave him be!"

"I don't really care if Wally likes the cold or not," Jim responded. "He's a mule, and he's going with me if I have to shoot him and drag him. Besides, this is a grown up talk, so just stay out of it." His tone was sharp.

Sarah broke into tears and ran to the house. "I thought you were nice," she cried as she fled.

Seeing the cause of his little girls tears before him, Tom left the saddle in a lunge. Jim was bowled over into the snow. When he came to his feet, Tom slugged him. Jim went sprawling again. This time, as he rose, he dove for Tom's legs only to have Tom sidestep and club him across the shoulders with both hands. Bundled as both men were, Jim was not injured, but when Tom pounced on his back and shoved his face into the drift he had plunged into, he could do nothing but flounder.

Tom leaned close to his ear and growled, "We may be partners, but don't you ever talk to my little girl like that again." He stood and shoved Jim's face into the drift again as he rose.

Tom strode to the house to find Sarah. She was sitting in the corner of the kitchen clutching Molly and petting Rufus.

Tears were running down her cheeks. Dinah was crouched beside her with her arm around Sarah's jerking shoulders.

"Daddy, that was mean! What Jim said was mean! He wouldn't really shoot Wally, would he? I like Wally and so do Rufus and Molly. Wally just doesn't like to be cold." She came into her daddy's arms and cried again.

"It's okay, pumpkin. I don't think he'd hurt Wally. Wally's a good old mule."

There was a tap at the door and it swung open a crack. "Tom, Dinah, can I talk to Sarah for a minute?"

"I don't want to talk to you!" Sarah blurted. "You were yelling at my daddy and said you were going to shoot Wally. That's not very nice." She scowled at Jim.

"That's what I wanted to talk to you about, Sarah." His voice was contrite. "You see, I was wrong to say what I said. I know you like Wally. Why? I'm not sure, but I wouldn't shoot Wally. I was angry. I'm still taking Wally with me, but I won't hurt him."

"Do you promise?" Sarah asked doubtfully.

"Yes, I promise." He looked at Tom. "You knew my conditions when I gave you half the ranch, Tom. The conditions haven't changed, but if you need some help, hire some more men. Take the expenses for them from my half if you want, but I need my freedom to ride when I need to ride."

Jim went quietly about gathering provisions to load on Wally, for travel. No apologies were offered between Tom and Jim.

Jim swung aboard a heavy black-and-white paint. It was a good horse and the one he had traded the dapple gray M/M horse for on his last fruitless foray. Taking Wally's lead rope he started to the south.

Dinah halted him before he left the yard. "Tom wanted me to tell you that if you pass through any towns and see any likely hands to send two or three this way. He thinks we'll need them."

"Will do." Jim touched his hat brim and rode from the ranch. He wasn't sure, but with Wally's long ears he worried they might freeze, so over the ears of the mule he slipped a pair of his socks. It looked silly, but Wally would keep his ears that way. Besides that, Wally seemed quite proud of his ear warmers. He twitched his ears forward and rolled his eyes to look at his ear coverings.

Twenty

In Concho Springs, Jim pulled up in front of the local café. He was cold, and some hot food and coffee sounded really good about now. He had spent two nights sleeping in snow caves and eating his own cooking. Knocking the snow from his pants and coat with his hat, Jim walked into the warm interior. A plump middle-aged woman poured him a mug of steaming coffee and set a platter of beef and a loaf of bread in front of him. There was already a bowl of butter, softened by the warmth of the room, on the table before him. "It's four bits," the woman stated flatly. "You can eat all you want, but you pay first." Jim fished out the required funds and dug in. Both the beef and bread were warm. Noticing a wedge of cheese further down the long table, he fished it in front of him. He cut several slices of cheese and added them to the thick sandwich he was building.

After eating his fill, Jim headed for the door. In the street there was laughter and the loud braying of a mule. Two cowhands were laughing at Wally and attempting to pull off the improvised ear warmers. Wally, of course, was protesting loudly. Each time one of the punchers would reach for his ears the big mule would lay them back snug against his head and strike at the offender with hoof or teeth. The paint had wisely moved as far away from the fracas as possible and stood watching disinterestedly.

One of the punchers was a little too slow in his retreat. While Wally missed with his teeth, the cowhand learned how hardheaded a mule really is when Wally butted him to the ground none too gently. The mule stepped onto the edge of the man's coat effectively pinning him to the ground and brayed loudly in victory. The second hand joined the onlookers in loud guffaws, once he was sure his coconspirator was uninjured.

Jim stepped into the middle of the commotion. He placed a hand on Wally's muzzle and backed him up from where he held the unfortunate prankster pinned to the ground. "You two have nothing better to do than to pick on a poor dumb beast? Why, I think you frightened poor Wally out of a year's growth."

"Sorry, mister," the puncher who had been dumped onto the ground replied. "We was just having some fun. I ain't so sure that mule's as dumb as he looks, though. He knowed how far his lead rope would reach and suckered me in too close." He chuckled good-naturedly as he wiped the snow and mud from his clothing.

His partner spoke. "I reckon that's what comes when you got no cows to punch. Me and Curly just couldn't help ourselves. Them ear socks on that ole mule was just too funny to pass up."

Curly retrieved his hat from where it had fallen and plunked it onto his head, which had no more hair then a billiard ball. "I reckon Sandy's right, mister. We should've drifted south some time ago, but we was more interested in spending our earnings than earning our spendings if you catch my meaning."

"You two hunting work?"

"Sure," they both responded. "But who's hiring?"

"Meet me over to the saloon and I'll fill you in. In the meantime I need to get my animals stabled for the night and find myself a place to rest up. Give me about a half hour and I'll meet you there."

Jim found the two men at a table drinking coffee laced with a shot of whiskey. As long as they were not going back out into the cold, it was not dangerous to do, but anyone who drank liquor while out in the cold was inviting death. The alcohol allowed the capillaries in the body to open and let warm blood flow to the surface. Outside, during cold weather, that heat was quickly dissipated causing hypothermia and death. Jim poured a cup of coffee from the pot on the table and sipped it appreciatively. He added no spirits to his own mug.

"You two got outfits?" Jim asked.

"Horses, saddles, guns, and clothes. What else is there?" replied Sandy with a grin. His boyish face shone with a joy for life beneath the straw-colored hair.

"Oh, I don't know, maybe a pack animal and some gear for the trail. The man I'm sending you to will work you hard, but you won't go hungry and the bunks are warm."

Curly was a little more practical than the sandy-haired puncher who was his saddle partner. "We was planning to ride south with the snow but we never made it. I reckon our outfits are pretty slim." Curly spoke quietly. "The fact is we need the job and we ain't scared of work. We're just not from the area, and the old hands keep the jobs and the new ones get culled. We just didn't breeze south as soon as we should've."

"Well, Wally likes you and he's a pretty good judge of character. I figure you two will earn your keep."

"Wally? You mean that flop-eared mule? What makes you think he likes us?" Sandy looked puzzled.

"That's pretty simple," laughed his partner. "If he didn't like us, he'd 'ave stepped on me instead of my coat like he done. Ain't that about so?"

"You got that right. Now what do you need for a three-day ride?"

The men talked over the details and made arrangements for Sandy and Curly to pick up an outfit. Jim gave them directions to the Lazy H and some guidance for the cold weather. Being from further south, they were unfamiliar with some of the information and listened intently. They ate their fill at the café and separated with Jim going over the directions one last time and giving them sufficient funds for an outfit.

The next morning Jim saw Curly and Sandy off and hung around Concho Springs trying to learn any information he could regarding the men he sought. The saloon seemed a likely place to find information, so, after lunch, he found a spot near the end of the bar to watch and listen. His order of a sarsaparilla drew a strange look but no comment from the barkeep. The soda was produced along with a mug, which the bartender poured it into.

It was still early, so Jim struck up a conversation with the bartender to pass the time. The man was friendly and enjoyed talking rather than listening to drunks.

I'm glad to see them two boys finding work. "They're a good enough sort. A bit rowdy, but not a bad type."

"Any more like them lounging about?"

"There're some lounging about but not their type. Those that're still loafing are the trouble-hunting type. Hardly worth their thirty a month."

As if to emphasize his point, two men pushed into the saloon with a truculent swagger. The bartender was already moving their direction when the more vicious of the two slammed his hand on the bar. "What's a man gotta do to get a drink around here?" he demanded.

"Yeah," his companion sneered. "We done been at this bar a whole ten seconds without no whiskey. A man would think we wasn't welcome."

The bartender was nonplussed. "Everybody is welcome here," he said. "Some are welcome to come in and others are welcome to leave. Now what's your pleasure?"

"Rye," growled the first man. "And leave the bottle, Me'n Frank are celebrating."

"You and Frank are celebrating? Good for you. It's a dollar for the bottle." The bartender smiled and held out his hand for the coin before relinquishing the bottle.

The truculent pair took their bottle and glasses and retired to a table. Shedding their coats and gloves—the saloon was warm—they began their "celebrating." The bartender polished the bar back toward Jim.

"Case in point," he muttered when close enough for Jim to hear. "They've been fired from most of the outfits around here. They seem to have money but not from any legitimate source you can find. By the way, most folks here abouts call me Dave. Easier on my ears than 'bottles,' 'barkeep,' and so on."

More customers came in as the day drew on, and Dave meandered away to serve them. There were a couple of local merchants, a drummer who had been trapped by the snow, a local rancher, and others. Talk welled up and a thick haze began to grow and fill the air with smoke from the cigars, pipes, and cigarettes. It was over the growing din of arriving customers and talk that Jim heard the grating voice of Frank's companion.

"I'd of shot that nag if it'd been me, but Curly just laughs it off and him and Sandy ride out with a nice outfit. Sold their pride I'd say! Why, Frank, me'n you ought to go see if 'n they'd share their good fortune with us. Or maybe we should see if that man would pay us not to shoot that stupid mule."

"That sounds like a right good idea," Frank chimed in. The two rose to carry out their plan not realizing that the man they intended to bulldoze into paying them was the man in the shadows at the end of the bar.

"I don't think so." Jim's voice was deceptively mild. "You two just sit down and finish your celebration and forget about your grand ideas. I hired them boys, and I don't like people harassing my hands. As for Wally, he's a mite smarter than some people I know. I'll save you some trouble with him. If you were to point a gun at him, he's likely to bite your hand off and stomp your guts out. Besides, I promised to bring him back home safe and sound, so I don't think I'll let you try." Jim's coat was off and his hands hung negligently at his sides.

"Could be you don't know who you're talking to, mule man! My name's Jack Slade, and my partner's Frank Yantz." Both men faced Jim and moved apart. They crouched menacingly, hands hovering near the butts of their guns.

"That's nice," Jim responded with an air of indifference. "Everyone should have one."

Slade looked confused. "One what?"

"A name," replied Jim. "It's good that you know it too. Why, even old Wally has a name and knows it. I guess you are as smart as a mule after all. By the way, the Cheyenne call me Can't Die."

"Well, the Cheyenne is wrong."

Men had scattered out of the line of fire as soon as Jim stepped from the shadows. While prudent, the move proved unnecessary. Slade and Yantz both reached for their guns and then looked into the blossoming flower of flame of first Jim's right-hand, then his left-hand Colt. Hours of practice and thousands of rounds of ammunition combined with Jim's natural ambidextrousness to send his bullets to their marks.

Struck in the chest just left of center, Jack was knocked from his feet as if by a huge fist. His heart was shredded by the soft lead that had smashed into his rib on the way into his chest. His gun fell from the holster it had failed to clear and his right hand clutched spasmodically at the floor. His eyes glazed in disbelief and death. Then demons howled and shrieked as they dragged the soul of another of Satan's children to their place in eternal blackness and torment.

Only a split second after Jack Slade crashed to the floor, Frank Yantz felt a searing pain in his chest. It felt like a sledge-hammer blow to his breastbone. Bullet and bone fragments tore lungs, heart, and arteries. His gun had barely cleared leather and he convulsively pulled the trigger while it was still tilted toward the floor. There was a pain in his right foot and he looked down at the hole in his boot wondering who had shot him in the foot. Then he toppled over onto his face and joined Jack Slade in the outer darkness.

Jim coolly reloaded both pistols then stepped back into the shadows at the end of the bar. The crowd returned to their former seats and somebody went for the undertaker. It was a stand-up shooting, and while the stranger in the shadows may have pushed it slightly, all who witnessed it saw Slade and Yantz make the first moves. No need to send someone for the sheriff twenty miles away in the county seat.

When the bartender returned to Jim's end of the bar, he brought two sarsaparillas. "I reckon they had it coming," he commented.

"I couldn't let them bad mouth my mule now could I?" Jim said dryly.

"I suppose not. Like I said, they had it coming to them. Not that there was any proof, but I figure there are some cattle herds a little safer without those two and probably a bit fewer drunks getting rolled. That's just my suspicions, though. Where'd you learn to shoot like that? I almost missed it and I was watching."

"My father taught me some. Some is from practice, and I've always been able to shoot almost equal with either hand. I'd better slip on out now. You got a back door? I don't feel much like talking to the gawkers."

"Sure." Dave pointed out the door, and as Jim reached for the coins to pay for his second sarsaparilla, Dave waved it aside. "On the house," he said. "In appreciation for good riddance to bad rubbish."

"Thanks, Dave." Jim slipped out the back door and walked around the building heading for the café down the street. He ate and headed for the hotel. There was little more he could learn here in Concho Springs, and he had no desire to be the object of curiosity.

The next morning the weather was few degrees warmer, and Wally had no need for his ear warmers. The sun rose bright and painted the eastern sky with brilliant pinks, purples, and oranges. Jim watched the sunrise while making tracks on the southbound trail. He was well within Wyoming by midday.

The Chinook winds were blowing in from the south bringing a midwinter warming a few weeks early. Jim felt that the warming trend would bring him good hunting. The snow softened and some melted making the trail sloppy and wet, but it was better than the bitter cold. The paint and even Wally seemed to perk up a bit.

~~✿~~ Twenty-one ~~✿~~

Jim rode into Pine Grove two days later and walked his horse down the slick, muddy street. The paint held his head high while brown mud and slush splashed onto his white stockings. Wally plodded along twitching his ears at each sound and swiveling his head to look about him.

They pulled up at the hitching rail in front of the marshal's office. In a burg like this, the lawman was sure to have noticed a group of several men traveling through. Whether he would share that information or not, one could never tell. You never knew unless you asked. With that thought in mind, Jim stepped up to the door.

The man facing Jim from over a large desk was tall, of medium build, and wore clothes in keeping with an honest lawman. His green eyes missed nothing as Jim entered. His red hair showed a touch of gray around the temples and the unruly locks framed a weather-darkened face that looked to have been hewn from walnut. He had noted the twin six-guns but had also seen that the hammer thongs were still in place holding the pistols securely. If the young man intended any foul play, he would have already slipped the thongs off.

"Howdy, young feller." His voice was a bit higher in pitch than expected but was friendly. "What brings you to our fair town and to the marshal's office no less?"

Jim decided that honesty was the best policy. "I'm looking for some men who may have passed through here in the past few weeks. About eight or nine of them from the account I got. They robbed a stage up to the north and killed the shotgun guard when he tried to keep them from roughing up a lady. He was unarmed when they shot him. They stole a mine payroll and robbed the passengers."

"I don't have much of a description other than one was riding a big black stud with white stockings. Another was riding a piebald gelding about fifteen hands tall. One was dressed like a Mexican and riding a roan-colored Appaloosa. They were wearing masks of course, so not much else. Someone said one of them had a scar over his left eyebrow." Jim had gotten the descriptions during his talks with Max.

"A group that size would get noticed if they stayed together. You fixing to follow them alone and get the payroll back? Them're long odds."

"I've faced long odds before. If I can, I'll get the payroll back where it belongs. If they are who I think they are, I have been looking for them, or some of them, for over a year now."

"You have a handle, son?" asked the lawman.

"James Harding. My family got wiped out by some of these skunks if it is who I hope it is. I'll recover the payroll, if I can, but this is kind of personal too."

"Harding? Seems to me I've heard that name. Killed a couple of fellers about a year and a half ago up near the border. Was shot last year by bandits and some feller was found by the posse hanged in the vicinity. Own the Lazy H up Montana way."

"Half owner," Jim corrected. "There was a family living there when I returned after living with the Cheyenne. The Cheyenne nursed me back to life when I was left for dead by those who slaughtered my family.

"Well, I couldn't run the family off. They'd done a lot of work on the place, so I gave them a partnership. It only seemed right. As for the rest, it sounds about right."

"Can't help you, son," stated the marshal.

Jim's lips formed into a hard line and his eyes narrowed. "Can't or won't?" he growled.

"Can't," stated the lawman flatly. He rose to his feet and was even bigger than Jim originally thought. "Don't get huffy with me, boy." The man was enormous. "If I meant won't, I would have said 'won't.' I said 'can't,' and that's what I meant. Now get out of here and cool off, or I'll toss you into a cell to cool off !" He pointed to the door.

Jim turned and stalked out the door."Me and my big mouth," he muttered. "Put my foot into it all the way up to the knee."

It was in the vicinity of Pine Grove that Max had lost the trail. The trail had been obliterated by snow somewhere west of town. Max had simply turned back at that point. Jerking loose the reins, Jim swung aboard the paint. He decided on a cup of coffee at the Spur. Maybe the barkeep would be a talker like Dave had been in Concho Springs. Besides, a hot cup of coffee sounded good even though the weather had warmed to about thirty-five degrees that day. He stabled his animals and stowed his gear with the hostler.

"It'll be safe enough. Nobody bothers with anything I stow. They figure they want their stuff safe if they gotta stow it themselves."

Jim nodded and paid extra for grain for horse and mule. "Make sure you give them both a good rubdown. They've been traveling a ways and could use it." Heading for the barn door, he noticed a piebald gelding still damp from travel.

Jim pointed to the piebald. "Looks like I'm not the only one traveling during the thaw."

"Nope. That fella got here just a bit ago. Mean-looking fella, but he rides good horseflesh."

Jim noted the brand, which looked like a mess of snakes in a wrestling match. A rustler or outlaw brand if he'd ever seen one. "He ride in alone?"

"Yeah, tonight anyway. He came in about a week back with another fella riding a big buckskin. Both seemed flush with cash, but the one on the buckskin seemed uneasy. The short fella on that there horse seemed set on a drunk. The other seemed like he was trying to ride herd on him without much success. They rode back out late that night. They woke me up stumbling around trying to saddle up. I'm s'prised they didn't fall into the manure pile, but they managed to mount up and ride out."

"Thanks," Jim replied. The piebald fit with his description and the time was about right. Maybe hunting was good after all. He smiled and whistled an off key tune as he made his way to the Spur. The only other patron was a short ferret-faced man with muttonchops and unruly brown hair. He was seated with his back to the wall and a bottle already two fingers beneath full on the table before him.

Jim moved to the end of the bar away from the surly-look-ing little man. He ordered coffee and paid two bits for the lunch counter. He sipped the coffee and built a sandwich of roast beef from the counter. Patience, not always his strong suit, was what he needed now. That and not being too obvious that he was watching weasel face slowly get drunk.

The hours passed and Weasel Face got surlier as the contents of the bottle grew less and less. He was not a happy nor a pleasant drunk. Jim watched as the man staggered out the back door to relieve himself. He shoved roughly past other patrons grumbling as he went.

Returning a few minutes later, he staggered into a young puncher making him spill his drink.

"Hey! Watch where you're going!" yelped the cowhand. He turned and shoved the drunk who stumbled back against a beam that supported the ceiling. "If you can't hold your liquor, you shouldn't drink." He turned back to the bar.

The small man moved away from the post and cursed. He pulled a wicked-looking knife from his belt. "Let's see who can hold their liquor," he slurred. He moved toward the puncher menacingly.

Jim started to move forward to intervene when a huge hand descended on the shoulder of Weasel Face. The man swiveled like the animal he resembled and found himself in the grip of the marshal. Before his muddled mind could comprehend what was happening, the marshal's other hand clamped down on this knife wrist. The pressure caused his fingers to loosen and the knife clattered to the floor.

"What's going on here, Dowes?" the marshal asked the bartender. "Why was this feller looking to cut up Pat?" He was still gripping the collar of the drunken former knife-wielder. The man squirmed to no effect in his grasp.

"Aww, 'twern't nothing, Marshal," responded Pat. "He just had a few too many."

"I reckon you better go sleep it off," the marshal addressed the drunk.

"No law dog tells me to go sleep it off ! I ain't done drinking yet!" Weasel Face slurred, his beady eyes tried to focus on the marshal through their bloodshot haze.

"I'm telling you that you are done, and now you can get out of town too." The big marshal tightened his grip.

"You can't—"

The marshal didn't allow time for the full protest. He slammed the former knife-wielder against a support post with enough force to shake dust from the rafters. "I can and I did! You get five minutes to be out of town or I'll toss you in jail and lose the key. And don't come back!" The marshal dragged his captive across the length of the barroom and dumped him unceremoniously into the street. It was barely dinnertime.

Weasel Face staggered to the livery barn muttering threats under his breath. He managed to saddle his horse and crawl into the saddle. The marshal and a few others, including Jim, watched him goad his horse out of town to the west. In his drunken state, he nearly toppled from the saddle and cussed his horse as if the animal was at fault. As the swaying figure disappeared, Jim retrieved his gear and saddled up to follow. Having no idea how far he would be traveling, he decided to take Wally with him just to be safe.

"Riding out already, huh?" queried the hostler. "Saw that other feller leave too. He seemed some put out."

"Yeah, I don't figure he was any too happy. He may need someone to follow along and make sure he gets home safe as much stump juice as he took in." Without further comment Jim swung aboard and rode into the night heading south. He planned to parallel the man on the piebald taking advantage of both the dark and his drunken state to cover the fact that he had an unknown shadow.

Jim swung around town and turned west. In the gloomy darkness he was able to pick out his quarry against the horizon. Following was easy due to the constant complaining by the drunk . When the complaining ceased, the night was split by a horribly out-of-tune version of some ribald song. The drunken concert continued for a couple of miles until the singer pulled his horse to a stop and slumped from the saddle.

Staggering to his feet, the man cursed his horse again then staggered a short distance off and vomited the contents of his stomach onto the ground. Jim pulled up in the shadows of a pine and watched as the man wiped bile from his mouth and stumbled back to his horse. From that point on, the man Jim was following rode in relative quiet. If he was aware he was being followed, he gave no indication of it.

It was almost three in the morning by Jim's estimation. Instead of growing colder, the temperature was actually warming up. A light fog rose from the melting snow giving the night an otherworldly glow.

Jim caught a faint whiff of wood smoke. Halting his horse, he sat silently waiting for a hail from the camp to give the exact location. He didn't have long to wait.

"Hey! Wake up you guys! Mikey's back!" shouted the man he was following. He wasn't quite sober yet. He had apparently stashed a pint in his coat pocket before leaving town and had imbibed of it as he rode.

Muttered curses rose from about two hundred yards away. "Why don't you tell the whole world where we are, you drunk!" was the response. "You weren't supposed to go nowhere without my say-so. Do that again and I'll kill you."

"I just wanted to get a snort," whined Weasel Face.

"I don't care what you want to get," was the growled response. "If that Vanderbilt fella was in town and recognized you, he'd of trailed you back and killed ya himself and saved me the trouble. I mean it, do it again and you're dead."

"Okay, Frank."

Talk quieted down, and shortly the outlaws rolled back into their bedrolls and slept.The lone exception was the Mexican who sat by the fire and added fuel. He had a bad feeling something was not as it should be. Somewhere from the night came a cry that sounded like a screech from the souls of the damned. He shuddered.

Jim heard the cougar and tied both horse and mule with a slipknot. He removed the lead rope from Wally's halter. He doubted the big cat would come this close to a human camp, but he wanted his animals to be able to escape if need be. They would stay where tied but could pull free if they gave a good tug.

Taking off his coat and gloves, Jim tied them on the saddle of the paint. He switched to his moccasins and added his boots and hat to the saddle. Taking his rifle, he slipped silently toward the now-quiet camp.

A thick fog hid his approach. He slid forward in silence inching ever closer. Whether Jacobs was here or not, he was not sure. If not, he would still do what he could to recover the mine payroll. A thief is a thief.

The screech came again, closer this time. The Mexican bandit built the fire higher and stared into the night. From the fog surrounding the camp came a shadow, an apparition. First there was nothing, then the fog swirled and a man seemed to just materialize. He stood silently with a rifle pointed directly at the bandit.

The fog seemed to carry the silent figure into the camp, the features not quite distinguishable. A pine knot full of pitch caught and flared up illuminating the face. Recognition was instantaneous for the Mexican. It was the face of a man he had seen shot down the year before while he was riding with another gang.

"Madre de Dios," he whispered.

"Not a sound," whispered Jim. "Nod your head for yes or shake it for no. Is Jacobs here?"

The terrified thief just stared. He mistook the shriek of the cougar for something not of this life. He was sure he was looking at one returned from the dead, perhaps seeking revenge.

"I'll ask again. Look at me. Is Jacobs here?"

It dawned on the thief that he needed to respond. Slowly, as if moving too quickly would make a noise and this "ghost" would respond by taking his soul for not obeying the command for silence, he shook his head no.

"Who is in charge? Point, do not speak."

Frank was pointed out. Jim prodded him with the muzzle of his rifle. Frank growled and sat up, rubbing his eyes. Jim stepped back to the edge of the fog. "What's the big idea, Sanchez?" Frank grumbled.

Sanchez pointed at Jim who was shrouded in fog. "He is a ghost. I see him killed." His eyes were as big as saucers as he stared. The fog swirled around Jim partially obscuring him.

"That rifle felt real enough. What ya want?" Frank's grumbling woke others and their stirrings woke the rest. Even Mikey stirred from his stupor. One started to reach for a gun when a voice from the fog stopped him. "I wouldn't do that. You asked what I wanted, Frank. Put the mine payroll into those saddlebags there and I'll just return it for you. Don't get between me and any of the others."

"If I don't? There are nine of us."

"There will be fewer of you and the law will be back on your trail."

Frank laughed to himself and stuffed the ill-gotten proceeds into a pair of saddlebags. "You got some nerve, but you won't get far. I'll play along."

Suddenly, there was an eerie cry of a cougar only a short way from camp followed by the terrified nickering of a horse and the harsh braying of a frightened mule.

The cougar snarled, gave its plaintive cry, and leapt for the paint horse. Both animals reared against the lines holding them, pulling loose. The cougar missed but turned quickly, unwilling to surrender a feast such as a horse or mule would provide.

Eyes wide with terror, both animals bolted, heading in the direction of their master, the cougar in pursuit. Being the fleeter of the two, the horse struck camp first. His master's coat, hat, and boots flopping with each racing step, added to his terror and speed to his flight. At the thunder of approaching hooves, everyone turned toward the sound, everyone but Jim. He snatched the saddlebags and ducked into the fog just as the horse burst into the firelight. The terrified horse raced through the camp bowling over men in his bid to escape the feared predator.

Wally reached the edge of the camp as the panther leapt onto his back. Feeling the weight of the big cat landing, the terrified mule reversed directions in a move that rivaled the best of cutting horses. The cougar lost his purchase and slid from the rump of the mule. Wally kicked the hunting cat. His flying heels sent the beast flying thirty feet to land in the midst of the camp already in disarray.

Sanchez was more convinced than ever that Jim was a ghost. He was calling on all the saints for protection for his immortal soul. Men were shouting, grabbing weapons, and cursing. Realizing he was in the midst of the hated man things, the cougar sought the safest route of escape. Mikey, brain still befuddled by booze, was the slowest to react and thus presented the obstacle of least resistance to the angry, frightened mountain lion. Leaping at the weasel-faced man, the cat's claws raked a furrow from scalp to chest opening wounds that emptied his lifeblood onto the ground.

Without intending to, the cougar ran straight for the outlaws' horses. Already nervous, the horses panicked and pulled loose from the picket line, racing away into the dark. There were more curses as the men in camp realized they were without horses or the money they had taken from their last holdup.

Jim trotted away from the scene in the fog. While he could not see what was taking place, he could picture it in his mind. He smiled slightly. Then he heard it; the clip-clop of hooves following him. He crouched and waited. The darkness and thick fog obscured the form that followed him. Then he recognized the long ears and doleful face of Wally. Once the danger was past, the mule sought his master. With a nose like a bloodhound, he had followed Jim's trail through the dense fog.

"Well, Wally, you old flop-eared goat, you sure arrived at that party in time to liven things up." Wally snorted in response and shoved his muzzle against Jim's shoulder. Jim patted Wally's cheek. He then rigged a bridle and checked the big mule for injury. Now that his fear was abated, Wally appeared no worse for wear. Jim rearranged what little was left of the packs and climbed aboard. Pointing east by instinct, he sought to put a few more miles behind them before resting.

The fog was still thick in many areas when Jim awakened, but the sun was already up and was dissipating the rest of it quickly. It was a matter of a few more hours of riding to get back to Pine Grove where he could unburden himself of the payroll before heading north to the Lazy H.

"You're doing pretty good, Wally," he said as they mean-dered toward town. "You've outlasted at least two horses, but you really need to leave them kitty cats alone. They keep getting closer to you every time." He whistled a tuneless melody and Wally cocked his ears to listen.

Knowing that his weight along with the packs made a big load for even a mule as strong as Wally, Jim climbed down and walked alongside to give the mule some rest. Not only that, but walking helped to keep the blood flowing. Even though it was warm for early January, his coat was somewhere behind him tied to the saddle of his now-departed horse. The exercise helped to keep him warm. He wasn't too worried about the gang of outlaws because he had heard their horses stampede when the cougar ran their way.

Jim had no way of knowing that there were two fewer high-waymen thanks to his visit to the Pullen gang's camp. Weasel Face, Mikey Flannery, bled to death from wounds received from the cougar. A shaken Miguel Sanchez still believed he had seen a ghost. If not, it was a sign, and he vowed to head south to his native Sonora as soon as he caught his Appaloosa. His mama and papa would be happy to see him, and he was a good vaquero. He could find a riding job. It was hard but honest work, and that ghost should not haunt him there.

Still an hour or so from town, there was a movement on their back trail. Jim stepped into the brush to wait. It was a thick stand of spruce that would hide both himself and Wally. The wall of trees partially concealed the trail as well. Jim slipped under the limbs that hung close to the ground and was able to watch in this way.

Ten minutes ticked slowly by. The sound of hoof strik-ing ground could be heard before anything could be seen. The horse would stop and crop grass then start again following the trail left by Jim. It would walk a few steps, stop, shake its head or crop some grass then trot a bit as if following but in no hurry. It was as if it was unguided.

As the thought hit him, the horse whickered questioningly. Before Jim could slide from under the trees and stop him, Wally brayed loudly in response. The answering whinny was accompanied by the sound of fast-approaching hooves. Jim looked in the direction of the advancing horse and recognized the paint immediately. Apparently, after getting over his panic, the animal decided it had no desire to be alone where a cougar might be hunting. Having grown accustomed to the company of the big mule, he had followed them, stopping occasionally to graze. Coat and boots were still in place, tied to the saddle. The hat was gone. A scratch in the saddle skirt from the cougar's claws and a small cut on his right flank seemed the only damage from the previous evening's excitement.

Jim cleaned the cut and applied some liniment he carried for just such things. He quickly donned his coat and switched back to his boots. Swinging aboard the paint, he put a lead rope onto Wally and trotted back to Pine Grove. It was hard to believe it had only been twenty-four hours since he rode in the first time.

"Marshal, I figure I should turn this over to you," Jim stated as he walked into the marshal's office. He laid the saddlebags on the big desk. "They decided to return it when I made the suggestion."

"Just like that, huh?"

"Not exactly, but close enough. By the time they gather their horses, I think they'll find other haunts." Thinking about what the Mexican in the gang had said, he had to laugh.

"Something funny?" The marshal looked confused.

"No, just I think one of them thought I was a haunt. I don't remember seeing his face before, though." Jim gave the marshal the name of the mine owners that the money belonged to. "I've no idea if it's all there or not, but it is a lot more of it than they had yesterday. I'm going to grab some food and some shuteye. Then, I think I better head back to the Lazy H. It seems to be getting colder by the minute, and it's a long ride home. So long, Marshal."

"So long."

Jim stabled his animals with the same instructions as before. Then he took care of his own needs. The next morning he headed north.

Twenty-two

The spring round up was a time of hard work and little else. From before sun up until after sundown, the men of the Lazy H were in the saddle. The lowing of cattle and the smell of seared hair and hide filled the air. Young animals recently changed from bull to steer went bawling back to their mamas with their new mark of ownership on their flanks. The heifers, likewise, rejoined the ever-increasing herd wearing a new design on them. "Mountain oysters" were part of the fare and were a welcome alternative or addition to beans.

Tom and Jim worked the men hard and themselves harder. The past fall Tom had arranged to supply the army with beef. A careful tally showed that, even though it had been a long winter, hard work and prudent planning had brought the herd through in good shape. Some loss was to be expected, but those losses were minimized through the efforts of all. Filling the Army contract and supplying several small mining towns would make this a profitable year.

"Well, Tom, it looks like we had a good crop of calves. Most of the stock looks pretty fat and sassy," Jim observed late one night. "Especially for the winter we had."

"We lost some during that storm over Christmas. A few more here and there. The wolves took some too. Gonna have to watch the calves or they'll turn our profits into losses. Two or three packs can kill a lot of stock. Even one pack is too much.

"Do you figure we have that many around?" Jim queried.

"Not sure, but we found kills scattered over a pretty good range. They find cows easier pickings than elk or deer, and you know what they do. They'll kill two, three, even four calves a day."

Curly rode up to the chuck wagon for some coffee. "I seen some shadows moving quiet like out there. A couple of the big bulls are edgy." It seemed to be confirmation of their concerns about predators.

"Keep a sharp eye," Tom told him. "Try to keep them away from the herd. Don't shoot unless you really have to though, otherwise we'll be rounding all them critters up again."

Curly nodded. Finishing his coffee, he grabbed a couple of bear signs and headed back to the herd. As he rode out the plaintive howl of a wolf split the night. It was far off in the mountains but was answered almost immediately by one closer to the herd.

As vigilant as everyone had been, there were still dead cattle the next morning. A cow and her heifer calf had somehow wandered outside the protective company of the herd. The wolves had eaten their fill and vanished before full light. Both carcasses were dragged as far from the holding grounds as possible. The loss of any cattle was more than a cattleman wanted to permit. The loss of both a cow and a heifer meant exponential losses.

The sunrise streaked the eastern horizon with an orange glow that turned to purples and pinks. Then the bright yellow orb climbed about the horizon to bathe the men and cattle of the

Lazy H with its first soft light of the day. Suddenly, a rider came hurtling toward them. He burst from a copse of trees, south of the herd, he had just ridden into a few minutes before.

"Injuns!" he shouted. He pointed to the trees. His horse slid to a halt and the young puncher yanked his rifle from the boot as he leaped from the animal's back. A couple of the other hands looked around anxiously and took up their own rifles.

Jim stood quietly looking in the indicated direction. Sure enough, a line of riders came slowly from the wood line toward the cow camp. Their bronzed bodies gleamed in the morning sunlight. Sitting erect in their saddles, they advanced with the dignity of the lords of the prairie that they were.

"Sit quiet all of you," Jim instructed. "Hey, Tom, keep the boys here and keep them calm. I'll be back in a few minutes."

"Where you going?" Tom asked.

Jim smiled and pointed in the direction of the approaching riders. "Why, out to say 'howdy' and welcome our guests."

Jim swung up and touched his heels to the bay gelding he was riding this day. He had recognized the Cheyenne style of clothing even from the distance. While not guaranteed he was pretty sure what band they were, he trotted forward to meet them.

"Two Bears, my friend!" Jim shouted the greeting in Cheyenne. He recognized the man who a few years before had saved his life.

"Can't Die, it is you!" The chief's pleasure was apparent to any who knew how to read his stoic face. "So how is the son of my old friend?"

"I'm feeling well enough to wrestle a bear. And you, my friend? I have not seen you in many moons."

The two conversed as they rode toward the chuck wagon. Two Bears spoke of battles and hunts and Jim of his quest and the ranch. He told of the wolves and the devastation they could wreak on his herds.

"The wolves have no buffalo to hunt," the Cheyenne chieftain observed. "White men slaughtered them for their hides and left their meat to rot. Now the wolves, like people, must survive without the great herds. The wolves have found your cattle to be slow and stupid, very easy to hunt. I fear they too will go the way of the buffalo."

"That may be so," Jim conceded. It was true. Cows were easier for wolves to kill than the great shaggy buffalo. They were also slower than the deer or elk that wolves normally preyed on. As much as he hated to lose cattle to the depredations of wolves, he knew it would be a great loss to see them gone forever. "Someday the white men must learn to live in harmony with the earth he has been given. Until then we must protect our cattle or the wolves will grow fat while our little ones go hungry."

The two loped ahead of the rest of the band to the cow camp. "Tom, you remember Two Bears, don't you? Boys, this is Two Bears. He's a friend. He and his people saved my life. Cookie, could you get him a cup of coffee please."

The band of Cheyenne was traveling north to their summer hunting grounds, but so far hunting had not been bountiful. Buffalo were disappearing due to hide-hunting, and with more domestic animals in the area, other game was more scarce and wary. The hard winter had also taken its toll on wild game. A thought came to Jim.

"Would twenty or thirty steers help feed your young ones and your ones with snow in their hair? I cannot let the wolves kill my cows. If your hunters can drive the wolves from here or kill them, I will give you thirty steers."

"Jim, thirty steers?" Tom asked quickly. "That's a lot of beef!"

"Just a second, Tom. This could work for them and us. Your hunters could easily do that." The last statement was addressed to Two Bears.

"I will talk to my people. The coffee was good. It is good to see you again, Can't Die." He sat silently for a moment, contemplating. "Perhaps, hunting has been bad and even a dumb cow is meat."

When the Indians had left the hands who had sat nervously watching the interaction, now started peppering their bosses with questions. The one at the top of everyone's mind was, "Are they hostile?"

Jim laughed at that one. "I suppose they can be if you offend them or take a potshot at them. For now, this band is peaceful to us. Some of the young bucks may get some ideas, though, so don't provoke them."

"Now, Tom, about those thirty steers. The way I see it, we lost two head last night, a cow and a heifer. That makes the loss even greater. That's four head next spring if you count their calves. Who knows how many we have lost on other nights in other places? I don' think we have just one pack either. The thirty steers is less than we will lose in just a few nights. My father and I never denied them a few head for their families anyway. This way, for less than we would lose to wolves, we get rid of the wolves and let those Cheyenne keep their pride. That and we give them steers, not breeding stock."

Tom smiled. "Well, when you put it that way, it makes good business sense."

The band of Cheyenne moved north past the holding grounds a few miles. There they camped. Two Bears gathered the council and told them of Jim's offer. "Our hunts have produced little and our young grow thin with hunger. While

Can't Die would not deny us a few beeves, this would put much meat in our pots."

"The wolf is a brother to us. Shall we deny him food? Shall we drive him from this land?" a young warrior asked.

An older brave spoke. "Can't Die, as his father before him, has allowed us to hunt and cross this land without having to fight. The Blackfoot fought his father and were driven from this land. The Cheyenne learned from fighting what the Black-foot did not. It is better to live with the white man and his family here in peace than to fight to cross this land. We can drive the wolf from the range to Blackfoot territory. There they can take food from the Blackfoot that our enemy may grow weak. The game will return when the wolf is gone and even a dumb cow is meat."

"It is charity," cried out another brave. He was young and full of bravado. "Are we all women?"

Standing Buffalo spoke now. "Have you tried to chase a wolf, Red Hawk? The wolf is cunning and does not like to leave where it is. When it finds food and water, it guards its home, but it can be driven out. It is not charity for Can't Die to trade cows for ridding this area of the wolf. We could hunt and kill them, but even that would not be easy. Can't Die would not let our little ones go hungry, but neither would he insult us by offering charity like we are children or old women." The low guttural tones of the Cheyenne language continued into the night. In the end the council broke up with no resolution.

The hunters scattered into the morning chill. With buffalo mostly gone, they had been hard-pressed to provide more than the daily needs of the traveling band of Cheyenne. Today, due to the deer and elk sharing the haystacks with the cattle, the hunt netted two young bull elk. There were also three large mule deer.

The hunting parties also saw the scattered bones of dozens of cattle, deer, and elk, all victims of the marauding wolf packs. That night, with the reports from the hunters, it was decided to take Jim's offer.

Standing Buffalo rode with his father to meet with Tom and Jim. When he spotted his friend two hundred yards away, Standing Buffalo raced ahead of his father. He rushed straight for Jim who was riding Buck this morning. Dropping to the side of his horse, Standing Buffalo leaned far out and slapped the ground. A puff of dust rose and Jim touched his heels to the ribs of his horse.

Buck lunged into a full gallop and Jim raced toward the approaching rider. He too leaned out and slapped the ground, then grabbed the saddle horn and dropped from the saddle. His feet struck the ground while he retained his grip on the horn and he vaulted back into the saddle. Standing Buffalo repeated the move, and the horses drew abreast. Both men pulled their horses to a rump-sliding halt, laughing like mad men they dove at one another. The horses pranced about raising dust and obscuring the two from view.

Never quite sure of what his partner might do in some situations, Tom followed cautiously. From the opposite direction, Two Bears maintained his dignified pace. Arriving at about the same time, Tom and Two Bears found the two young men wrestling on the ground laughing like children. At his father's approach, Standing Buffalo did his best to look stoic and dignified, but neither young man could erase the grins from their faces.

"Humph! You behave like cougar cubs when you meet," the old warrior admonished sternly, but his eyes glittered with amusement. It is good to be young, he thought. He also knew, had others from the tribe been present, Standing Buffalo would have behaved with all the dignity of his position.

"Ha! No cougar cub can wrestle like Standing Buffalo," Jim responded.

Tom looked at the two dusty figures standing on the ground. He turned his eyes heavenward then glanced at Two Bears. He shrugged his shoulders. "I reckon you can't tame them any more than you could a cougar cub," he remarked to the mounted warrior. He had learned some of the Cheyenne language from Jim. "The difference is, if you cook it right, you can eat a cougar," he concluded in English.

"True," Two Bears smiled in agreement.

The four returned to the chuck wagon and had coffee while Jim and Tom were informed of the council's decision. "That will be good for all of us," Tom said. After figuring out the wisdom of this arrangement, he was glad to hear that it had been agreed to. How they planned to carry it out he had no idea, but he had confidence they would be successful. They would do it without the poisons that some cattlemen were now using. Poisoning the wolves went against everything Tom and Jim believed. They had seen animals die that way and refused to use such horrible techniques regardless of the losses.

Two Bears and Standing Buffalo rose to leave. They had work to do to prepare for the task of driving wolves from this territory. "Can't Die, you will come and learn our way to deal with the wolf. If you do, they will remain gone, and when next my people return, there will be much game and fat cows." Two Bears looked at the young rancher.

"Can you spare me, Tom?" Jim asked his partner.

Tom gave it some thought before replying. While he needed the help, keeping predators at bay was important. If it could be done without the need to hire a hunter, it might make up for the loss of one man at this stage of the roundup. "I think we can spare you for now. Just make sure them wolves are gone. They're moving closer to the herd every night, and Curly found a big steer back in the breaks that they got."

"Okay, Tom. I'll be back once we get the job done."

Buck was a horse that he knew would not flinch around wolves. A cougar, perhaps, but for some reason wolves did not terrify him. He dabbed a loop on a sturdy roan to take as a spare mount.

The three men trotted their horses in the direction of the Indian encampment. Jim was anxious to renew some friend- ships. One he especially looked forward to was with Gray Owl. The old shaman's wit was what buoyed Jim many times during his two-year recovery. There were also several young braves and at least one young maiden.

The reception of Can't Die was warm and boisterous. Hunters returned again after a moderately successful hunt and joined in the reverie. That night the methods of moving the wolf packs were discussed. The hunting parties had been instructed to watch for signs of the wolves while out and repeated signs of at least two packs and possibly one or two others. Some of the more experienced hunters had tracked the huge beasts partway into the valleys at the base of the moun- tains. They did not follow them to their den areas. The time was not yet for that. Besides, while wolves would not normally attack a healthy man, if their dens were intruded on by one man, the man stood little chance of survival.

"First," began Strong Eagle, a hunter known for his uncanny way with animals, "you must learn to talk to the wolf. Some know and others will learn. Then we will tell the wolf he must go to other hunting grounds where there are no white eyes. We must convince them to take their young and go. It will not be easy for they have much food here, but we shall do it."

All accepted Strong Eagle's assessment. All knew of his mysterious, almost magical exploits. Jim himself had seen Strong Eagle "talk" a huge bull moose to within a few yards of where the hunter stood and allow Strong Eagle to approach. The brave continued to talk softly to the bull moose as he walked around the huge animal, finally reaching out and touching it gently on its ugly snout.

When questioned about it, Strong Eagle said he simply told the moose he did not want his meat or hide or antlers. He said that after they talked he told the moose to go before the other hunters decided they wanted those things. Many believed he could actually talk to the forest creatures somehow.

The present problem sounded simple to overcome from the hunter's statements, but none seemed to know how to "speak wolf," none but perhaps Strong Eagle. "I will teach those who come with me to tell the wolf to go. You too, Can't Die, must learn to speak like a hunting wolf. I will need four other braves who can be spared from hunting. Each day after the hunt they will learn the wolf's language. When they learn it, we will go and talk to the packs." Four young braves quickly volunteered to help.

For the next week, every minute not spent hunting was spent in training with Strong Eagle. "You must become a wolf," he would tell them as they attempted to mimic yips and snarls as well as the howl of the great gray beasts. "Each sound means something. Do not be so foolish as to think you will fool the wolf. He knows you are not one of his own, but if you talk to him in his tongue, he will listen. If he thought you were another wolf rather than a man who talks to him, he would kill you for invading his territory."

Two of the braves were unable to vocalize to Strong Eagle's standards, so they were told to be silent while the other two and Jim continued. At the end of that week, Strong Eagle was satisfied. He had not only taught the three young men to mimic the wolf to near perfection but had also taught them how to throw their voices like a ventriloquist. This delighted them as much as learning to "talk" to the wolves. It was great sport to talk to a friend from the forest and approach them from the opposite direction from where their voices came. The last night, as they talked, the wolves howled back and came close to the village to see who spoke their language. "Tomorrow we go and talk to them," Strong Eagle said when he heard howls and saw the yellow eyes at the edge of the firelight.

The two young warriors whose voices were not good enough to learn the language of the wolf had not been idle. While the others howled and yipped or growled, they had been busy preparing arrows with heavy blunted tips. They had also been provided with wolf hides to wear in their role. They were not to crawl and attempt to look like a regular wolf, but to stand with the wolf hide for a covering. The wolf knew their kind did not walk on two legs, so this along with the calls of the other four men would serve to both arouse their curiosity and increase their wariness of this new wolf-man creature.

These two would carry heavy hunting bows and several of the blunted arrows. While not dangerous to the wolf, the arrows would deliver a painful blow to a wolf that got too close. That the two-legged wolf-man creatures could cause pain from a distance would aid in driving them form the area.

The long grass of the meadow was heavy with dew and tendrils of fog drifted close to the cool ground. The six men, led by Strong Eagle, started toward the mountain valley where one of the packs had been located. They trotted silently for half an hour then walked, then trotted again. In this way they swiftly put miles behind them. Shortly after sunrise they were drawing close to the den area and slowed their pace.

The fog began to burn off, and they could hear the soft padding of several animals just out of view. A shadow moved on the edge of the haze. Low growls penetrated the fog from all sides. The men halted.

Strong Eagle spoke quietly into the still morning air. "Brother Wolf," he called softly in Cheyenne. "We do not come as enemies but as brothers." He yipped softly a few times, then barked, and followed with a deep growl.

A huge black shadow materialized out of the fog not twenty yards distant. There was a rumbling growl as the hundred-and-thirty-pound wolf bared its teeth menacingly. The only weapons carried were personal knives, tomahawks, and the bows with blunted arrows carried by those wearing the wolf skins.

Strong Eagle showed no fear. He growled more fiercely and stepped toward the wolf. Then he said again in a quiet voice, "Brother Wolf, we have not come as enemies." Then to one of the braves he whispered, "If I tell you, Great Bear, shoot him in the belly. Now we must talk." A shot in the belly by one of the arrows would be extremely painful to the wolf but would do no real damage. To those who had learned to mimic the wolf, he said, "When I howl, you howl too. They must understand we do not mean them harm nor do we fear them."

Again the yips and snarls. The wolf continued to bare its teeth. The huge creature snarled and moved back and forth but came no nearer. Two or three others came from the fog and watched the scene.

Great Bear had an arrow nocked and drew his bow. He was aptly named, for he was a huge bear of a young man. Powerful of shoulder and chest and an excellent shot with his bow, he could hold the bow at full draw for five minutes and still hit his target. He waited for his signal.

Strong Eagle continued snarling and began snapping his teeth together, twisting his head from side to side. He moved forward. The black wolf snarled and lunged forward three steps then retreated, unsure of this man thing that talked like a wolf. "When he charges again, I will point at him, shoot then."

Tense seconds passed as the snarling from both quarters continued. Suddenly, the wolf sprang and Strong Eagle pointed. The blunt arrow struck home eliciting a yelp from the wolf that was knocked to the ground by the powerful blow. Before it could recover its senses, Strong Eagle sprang astride the wolf bearing it to the ground. He clamped his hands around the wolf's snout holding the powerful jaws closed. Throwing back his head, he howled into the morning air. Three other human voices joined in, and the wolves that had come closer to watch fled.

"Brother Wolf, you must leave this place. You cannot come back. Flee over the mountains." Strong Eagle whispered in the ear of the wolf. As the soft voice of Strong Eagle continued, the struggles of the pinned wolf subsided. The three young men continued their cacophony of howls and snarls.

Great Bear retrieved his arrow and backed away in awe as Strong Eagle rose allowing the huge shaggy beast to rise as well. The wolf snarled slightly then spun and dashed into the forest. A howl was heard then several receding footsteps including the young could be made out. The pack abandoned the den area and headed up the valley toward a pass that would take them into Idaho. Borders meant nothing to a wolf.

Late that night, thirty miles away, the howl of a huge black wolf announced the end of a successful hunt. After feasting on elk, the pack would continue deeper into the mountains and away from those strange wolf-man creatures. They could not be merely men for had not the one called him brother wolf? It did not matter. Their bellies were full, and wolves, like all wild creatures, do not contemplate such things. That is the domain of man. Later that night, men gathered around a large fire and retold the story. Strong Eagle left the story-telling to the younger warriors and walked silently into the forest. There he squatted in the moonlight to recount in his own mind what had happened and how well things had gone. Let the young ones celebrate for now. He would tell his version of the story later. For now he would commune with the wild things. Now he would listen to the night and give thought to their next objective.

A short time later, soft footsteps intruded on his thoughts. "Come, join me, Can't Die," he said without looking around. "It was a good day, but not all wolves will show wisdom like those today."

Jim smiled in the dark. He had not been particularly careful about making noise, but he still moved quietly. "How did you know it was me?" he asked. He moved so he was facing the Cheyenne warrior and sat on the ground.

"You move quietly, almost silently, but you still do not move like a Cheyenne. I have heard your steps. Besides, the mink told me it was a white man approaching. What other white man is in our village?"

Jim had seen many inexplicable things during his time with the Cheyenne. He was not sure if Strong Eagle was serious or not about the mink, but he knew that different people's footsteps sounded different. As for the mink, after what happened with the moose years before and the wolves today, he was not convinced it was beyond the realm of possibility.

"They will want you to tell the story too. In Great Bear's version his arrow had no effect and you stared the wolf into submission. In Diving Hawk's we wrestled the whole pack. They are great stories, but maybe you should set it straight. The others, I think, will have their telling as well. What really happened is an even better story. You should tell it."

"Why not you, Can't Die?"

"It is your story to tell, my friend. Come. They would hear from the one who talks to wolves, and listens to minks."

Strong Eagle smiled and the two walked back to the council fire. Silence fell as he began to recount the day's events. He spoke of the travel and the wolves in the mist. He held them all in rapt wonder as he drew them into the story. He gave full credit to Great Bear for his shot that stunned the great wolf. Not only was Strong Eagle reputed to be able to talk to animals and they to him, but also was an accomplished storyteller. When he finished, he had taken his spellbound audience on the hunt with them. "The great wolf showed that he had the wisdom to lead his pack. They have gone, led by a great leader."

Where most warriors would have taken credit for driving the wolves out, seeking honor, Strong Eagle gave credit to others including the wolf. All knew he downplayed his part and he was honored all the more for it.

The next day they took provisions for a week and set out to locate the other packs and attempt to move them out too.

Each man rode one of his favorite war ponies. Strong Eagle's words proved prophetic. The second pack of wolves was led by a huge light gray brute with several battle scars on his shoulders and face. One ear was split making a V-shaped notch.

The first contact with the pack broke off only after Great Bear and Diving Hawk had unleashed a barrage of painful missiles from their bows. Both wolves and men withdrew warily.

"This wolf does not want to talk," Strong Eagle said that evening. "He wants to fight. He carries the scars of many battles and wonders what can hurt him. His pack has killed the cougar and driven the bear from his meal. He does not understand the white man is neither of these. We shall try again tomorrow, after I talk to the wind."

That night a soft rain fell. While the six men slept, the ground grew soft and muddy. Sound was covered and movements were quiet. The fire was built up and the horses brought in close for the night. With the wolves nearby, nobody wanted to lose their horse to them.

The men set out in the morning drizzle. Mud splattered their legs and caked their moccasins as they trotted toward the den area. "Today their leader will listen, or I will kill him and tell the rest to go."

Unlike the black wolf from days before, when the shaggy gray wolf rushed forward, he did not stop. It was not a feint but an attack. Snarling his own wolflike battle sounds, Strong Eagle sprang to meet the beast. The wolf dove for the throat but Strong Eagle dodged to the side, striking the wolf with both arms in passing.

Both combatants crouched and circled. Wolf and man both snapped their jaws in warning, but as yet Strong Eagle had not drawn his knife. Instead he spoke again. "I do not wish to kill you, strong warrior, but you must leave or you will all be hunted and killed." He growled and barked again at the wolf.

This time it was Strong Eagle who attacked. He rushed forward and kicked at the wolf, but the wolf was used to being kicked at by animals like elk or deer and dodged the foot easily. The ground was slippery from the rain and Strong Eagle slid losing his balance. As he fell to the ground, the wolf spun and leapt for his throat.

Fearing the death of their leader, Great Bear bent his bow to full draw, but even if he released the arrow, it would not be soon enough. Diving Hawk had the same thought but was even slower to react.

Knowing what his adversary would do when he fell, Strong Eagle had already prepared to meet the threat. His instinctive understanding and swift reflexes were already at work as the fangs of the wolf sought the soft flesh of this throat.

Swift as a striking serpent, his left hand grasped the tongue and lower jaw of the beast yanking the shaggy head sideways. He could feel the hot breath on his face, but the teeth missed his throat. His hold on the bottom jaw and tongue kept the wolf from closing his jaws around the hand that held it.

Rising to his feet, the Indian gripped the wolf by the hide of his shoulder and heaved the animal aside. Again he spoke and then barked and growled. His left hand was bleeding and the wolf's tongue was lacerated as well. Neither injury was serious, but both combatants had been blooded.

Men and wolves followed the battle as it moved closer to the tree line. Again the wolf sprang for Strong Eagle. This time, instead of evading the attack, he caught the wolf by the throat just behind the jaws with one hand and the fur of his belly with the other. He hoisted the animal into the air and turned toward a pine tree with broken limbs projecting from the trunk. "I am sorry, Brother Wolf," he said quietly. Then he impaled the brute on one of the limbs of the tree.

There was a yelp of pain as the limb tore through hide and flesh. Then the heavy body sagged. Strong Eagle released his hold but did not back away. Instead he stroked the scarred head of the wolf as the life drained from his body. "You are a great warrior," he told the wolf. "Your praises will be sung of by my people." The wolf whined and licked Strong Eagle's face. Then his eyes glazed over.

Strong Eagle took the body gently from the limb and carried it into the clearing. There he tilted back his head and let out a mournful howl. Both man and wolf joined in.

As he knelt beside the body of the fallen wolf, he began to chant in honor of the wolf's courage. A lone gray figure detached itself from those standing a short way off. The shaggy wolf, nearly as large as their fallen leader, padded quietly to Strong Eagle's side. The beast growled slightly then sniffed the still form on the ground. Strong Eagle seemed not to notice and continued his tribute to the warrior wolf.

After finishing the inspection of its now-dead leader, the wolf sat beside the chanting brave and tilted back his huge head adding a mournful howl to the keening of the human who seemed to mourn too. The leader of the men ended his mournful cries. The wolf beside him stopped as well. With moist eyes in his normally stoic face, he reached out and stroked the head of the new leader of the wolves. "Go and take your family from here. Go over the mountains. We will honor Gray Scar and tell our young of his strength and cunning. Now go!"

The wolf whined then turned and trotted away. One by one the shadows that had surrounded the men followed. A short time later a chorus of howls rose from the southwest. The wolf pack was on the move to their new home.

"We will bury him with honor in his den. Then we shall mark it as our own. The pack will leave and not come back. They will travel many days before they stop." They found the den proper and laid the animal respectfully within it. Then, like wild things, they marked the area the same way the wolf had before.

A week later the third pack was found. It was small, only about ten animals total, and was quickly driven from the area. Now the only howls heard on the Lazy H were those of the Cheyenne and one white man as they retold the story of Gray Scar, the warrior wolf.

The next morning the cattle were delivered to the Cheyenne camp. A small band of neighboring Cheyenne rode into the village on a visit. The group of five visiting hunters told of being attacked by a gang of about twelve white men. They had escaped, due in part to the drunken state of the whites. Their shots were wild and ineffective. When one of their pursuers fell drunkenly from his horse, the pursuit stopped and the hunters scattered into the forest losing themselves in the trees. They had heard one of the men called Jacobs.

Jim heard the name and was instantly attentive. He pulled one of the newcomers aside and asked questions. Could he describe the attackers? Where did it take place? Could they tell him where they might be heading?

The brave laughed. The whites had been such fools that he thought it fun to crawl close to them and taunt them. While he had no idea where they were going, he was able to describe men, horses, and location with exacting detail. He told how he had wormed his way back out of effective range and stood in plain view hurling insults and ridicule as they stumbled around trying to remount their nervous horses. Before the first one was successfully in the saddle, he had climbed aboard his waiting pony and left them far behind.

Jacobs, he had found him again. From the visiting hunter's description, there was no doubt it was him. Three days to the northwest, maybe four, and he would be on their trail again.

Jim thanked his hosts for both their hospitality and for ridding the range of wolves. He left the encampment and headed for the gathering. He needed supplies, and Buck had been ridden hard the past several days, so he would need a fresh horse along with the roan he was leading.

He rode into the holding area and turned back into the rope corral after swapping the saddle and bridle from him to the roan. He dabbed a loop on the pinto he had ridden during his Christmas excursion and was loading supplies onto him when Curly rode in for coffee.

"Glad you're back, boss. We can use help."

"I'm on my way out again, Curly. Sorry, but you'll have to get along without me!"

"Off again?" Curly was confused. "But you ain't hardly got back. Now that the wolves are gone, what is more important than finishing roundup?"

"Look, Curly, you work for me, not the other way around! It's personal business that can't wait," Jim retorted. "Tom knows what it is. It's part of our agreement."

As if summoned by the mention of his name, Tom trotted a leg-weary horse to the chuck wagon for coffee. Jim finished loading the pinto and swung astride the roan. The red horse pranced around eager to go. Tom eyed Jim disappointedly. He knew that eager light of hatred that was dancing in Jim's eyes. Their relationship had digressed into nothing more than a business venture, and he knew the conditions of their partnership.

"Riding out?" Tom knew the answer. "We could use you right now. It'd only be a few more days."

"That would make the trail a few days colder. I can't wait." Jim's tone was level.

"They've almost put you under more than once. One of these times they may succeed." It was an old argument, old and unsuccessful.

"Then you will have the whole ranch instead of a share." Jim's answer was spoken seriously.

Curly finished his coffee quickly and went to saddle a fresh mount before returning to work at the branding fire. This was not his business.

Tom shook his head solemnly. "I'd not want the ranch that way."

"Maybe not, but if it happens, you'll take it. Besides, according to the Cheyenne, I'm Can't Die, so I'm safe enough. It's them that need to worry." He wheeled his horse and rode out of camp. Tom looked after him and swore. That was something he rarely did. Dinah would box his ears good if she heard him.

⤳ Twenty-three ⤳

J im rode at a distance-consuming trot. The horses were in good shape and the travel was smooth. He covered fifty miles that day and bedded down in a small glade with only the stars for a roof. It was a new moon and the night was dark. A coyote began to yap close by. It was a stark contrast to the deep howl of the wolf that Jim had learned. Listening to the crickets and the coyotes, he drifted off to sleep.

The next two days passed in similar fashion: up before the sun, shaking the dew from his ground sheet, and get back on the trail. The fourth day began the same way, but Jim traveled much slower. The directions given to him brought him near the area of the encounter the Indians had had with Jacobs and the drunken outlaws.

Now Jim stayed deep under cover. His eyes never stopped scanning for any telltale sign of others in the area. He had to be the one to locate them, not the other way around. If they spotted him first, his Cheyenne name would mean nothing. They would not hesitate to kill him.

He had switched his boots for moccasins this morning and several times dropped from the saddle to scout silently ahead on foot. The day ended with no sign of the outlaws he sought.

He knew he must be close because the landmarks described by his informants were here. Tonight he would not chance a fire. On a dark night it would be far too easy to spot. Besides, he had hardtack and water. There was no need to cook.

He was restless that night. His quarry had to be close or at least some sign of them. Sleep eluded him and he climbed a small hillock and stared into the night.

A tiny sliver of moon climbed above the eastern horizon. Stars blinked at him from the black velvet of the night sky. Bats flitted to and fro, invisible in the night as they snatched moths and mosquitoes from the air. Somewhere nearby a rabbit squealed as the silent, master of the night skies' talons found their mark. The great horned owl lifted noiselessly back into the air clutching its evening meal tightly.

The clear mountain air allowed the stars to dust the sky like so many diamonds. Then Jim spotted one that seemed too low to the ground. It blinked out then came back into view again. Not only did it seem too low, but also it was alone in its position. He watched for several seconds. The star was the wrong color too. More yellow than the pinpricks of brilliant white of the other stars. "That's a fire," he whispered to himself.

Noting the position of the fire, Jim retreated down the hill to his dark camp. He could do nothing tonight but comforted himself with the thought that somewhere ahead he would find those he sought. The fire might be anyone, but he convinced himself it was Jacobs.

Morning could not come soon enough for Jim. Long before the last stars had disappeared from the sky he was in the saddle moving in the direction of the fire he spotted the night before. He would have to scout them carefully and make his plans, but he was close to his query. He was sure of it.

When still about two miles from where he had seen the fire the previous night, Jim circled toward the north seeking signs. He found no indication of a large party of horsemen. He continued scanning the ground. He turned back to the south and moved nearer where he had spotted twinkling eye of firelight. On this sweep he found a few smudges and a small partial hoof print.

Jim slipped from the saddle and studied the ground closely. As an accomplished tracker he could read the story easily. The size of the hoof and the length of the stride identified its maker as a burro. He found a boot print showing low heels and a wide flat sole. A prospector. The trail led toward the fire he had spotted the night before. Since the tracks had been made the day before, it stood to reason that it was this prospector and not the outlaws who had built last night's fire.

He mounted and followed the trail. The roan's ears pricked forward about a half mile farther down the trail. They twitched from side to side and then back forward. Jim patted the horse's neck reassuringly. Jim's ears picked up the sound. The soft contented hee-haw of a burro was followed by indistinguishable words spoken in a soothing manner. The sound was coming closer. Jim rode his horse to the side pulling the packhorse with him and waited. Perhaps this was not who he was looking for, but they may have some information he could use.

"C'mon, Nellie Mae, we won't go too far. Besides, when we get to a town, I'll buy you a good bait of corn and another of oats." The voice was old and filled with a coaxing gentleness. The burro brayed quietly in response.

Before the pair came into view, the burro stopped. "What's the matter, Nellie Mae?" the man asked quietly. It was almost as if he expected a response, but Nellie Mae was not Balaam's ass, so she could not speak to her master. "You stay put, young lady, and I'll go and see what's up ahead," her master whispered.

He slid a .56 caliber Spencer carbine from the pack on her back and slipped into the woods. The heavy boots he wore might be good for prospecting, but they were loud and clumsy for sneaking through the brush. Jim knew of Cheyenne children who were quieter while playing in the trees than this old prospector. He decided there was little danger from him and started his horses forward whistling slightly. Coming into sight of the burro, Jim halted. He knew the prospector—it had to be a prospector based on what the burro carried—was to his left and slightly behind him. The burro had stayed where she was without being tied, and Jim greeted her by tipping his hat and saying, "Well, hello, Nellie Mae. What a lovely day for a picnic, don't you think?"

The little donkey trotted up to the roan and brayed in response. The man had spoken her name, so he must be all right,[1] not like some who threw those loud noise makers that banged and flashed sparks and the smell of gunpowder at her feet. Nellie Mae did not know what fire crackers were called, but she knew she didn't like them. Their voices were harsh and mocking, but this man sounded nice. Surely it was safe for her to approach.

"Nellie Mae, you stay back from that claim jumper." The voice came from almost exactly where Jim thought it should. The little donkey stopped obediently. She turned her huge brown eyes toward her master's voice. "Now, you on the horse, what do you want? And don't you think you talking

---

1 The story of Balaam and his talking donkey is found in the Bible in Numbers chapter 22.

to my burro like you're old friends is gonna help none. I ain't seen you before and likely she ain't neither."

"No harm intended. I heard you call her by name and simply greeted her." Jim turned his horse slightly so he could see the man as he stepped from the brush.

The man was an old timer with cottony white hair. He was tall and thin but held the spencer in capable hands, or Jim missed his guess. A brown leather vest was worn over his faded brown woolen shirt, which was tucked lopsidedly into his buckskin trousers. His tattered felt hat was pushed to the back of his head. It almost matched the one that was perched on the burro's head except her ears poked up through two holes in the brim of hers. He was slightly bent from time spent hunched over a gold pan or shoveling gravel into a sluice box.

"I assure you, I am no claim jumper either," Jim stated. "But it has been several days since I've had company besides my horses. Smart as they might be, they are poor conversationalists."

The old man spat to the side and lowered his rifle. "Well, if you are a claim jumper, you can have the last one I worked. Not enough gold in it to fill a thimble. Nellie Mae and me was off in search of greener pastures. Been nigh on two months since I had any human company myself. Guess I'm getting a little itchidy when folks come along. Not sure what to think."

"Two months since you've seen another human. That must get pretty lonely."

"Yeah, well, it can, but Nellie Mae's good company. Besides, I said two months since I had human company not since I seen another human. Of course, that last batch was barely human and I stayed short of their company. They tried to shoot down some poor Injuns that was just riding through.

Course they was so drunk, the white men that is, they was so liquored up they couldn't've hit a bull in the butt with a bass fiddle. Neither Nellie nor me had any liking for meeting them, so we just stayed hid out 'til they was gone. That'd be just about a week ago or so. If 'n they was the only human company around, I'll do without."

The old man seemed hungry for company, and Jim was hunting information. The sun was near its zenith. "It's near enough time for a nooning. How you fixed for coffee, old timer?"

"Coffee? I been out of that for nigh onto three weeks. Sure could use a spot of it if you got some," the prospector responded hopefully. "Part of why I'm heading back to civilization. Man can rustle up his own grub if he knows what to look for, but coffee, that's something else entirely."

"Well, I've got plenty of coffee and some dried beef if you've got something to cook it up in."

The cotton-haired oldster walked off toward a small creek while Jim got a fire of dry wood going. While Jim dug out the coffee and dried beef, the prospector pulled a battered coffee pot and huge skillet from the pack on the donkey's back. He scooped water from the stream for coffee and pulled some wild onions to add to the beef and beans Jim was heating over the fire. "These'll give her some flavor."

"Thanks. By the way, most folks call me Jim. What's your handle?"

"Well, sonny, I been called a whole heap of things over the years, late for dinner usually wasn't among them, but folks of late call me Dusty. Usually I have a little dust when I hit town, so that's what they call me. Don't look like I'll have much this time around. Maybe then they'll call me Empty 'cause that's about what my poke will be." He laughed.

Dusty was hungry for conversation, and the midday rest drew on for hours. Jim steered the conversation to the outlaws he was hunting and was able to glean even more information. Their direction of travel, number in the party, and the fact that the last four men he sought were part of the group. Dusty talked and Jim listened. His father had taught him that you hear more if you listen than if you talk, so he listened well.

"Them yahoos stuck around too long, so Nellie and me decided it was time to skedaddle. They're probably still sleeping off their last drunk."

"I thought you said you saw them a week ago. How do you know they're still around?"

"I don't have to see 'em to see their sign, boy. I just keep out of sight and stay clear of 'em. Long as they stayed where they was, we had no problems."

"That makes sense. I'd hate to run across them unexpected like. Where are they holed up?"

Dusty gave the location of the outlaw camp and a fairly good description of the surrounding terrain.

"Danged if I ain't jabbered the afternoon away. Aw well, I've nowhere special to be. Looks as likely spot to nest for the night as any," Dusty said glancing up at the sky. He went to his burro and removed her pack leaving her free to graze and roam around. "Better'n a watch dog," Dusty quipped.

The two men went about setting up camp for the night. Dusty shot a turkey that was drinking at the creek and they dined well that night. After the meal the two men swapped more information about trails and weather conditions. Dusty filled his pipe with pungent tobacco and lit it with a brand from the fire. That done he regaled Jim with stories of past strikes and boomtowns. "Why I even heard tell of some way to get the gold out of the ground without making a huge mess of the land nor fouling the creek. That'd be good. Just clean up the color and leave everything else the way you found it." When asked, he couldn't remember exactly where he had heard such, but he was sure he had.

The next morning the men parted. Jim gave Dusty half of his coffee and watched as he walked down the trail with Nellie Mae following behind. He smiled and turned the roan in the direction of the outlaw camp. Jim made an early camp three or four miles from where he suspected the outlaw camp to be. Leaving his horses picketed on the rich grass in a creek bottom, he stashed his gear and switched from his riding clothes to some well-worn buckskins. The natural coloring blended well with his surroundings, and brush did not snag on them like it would wool or even cotton. He took a piece of charcoal he carried in his saddlebags and smudged some of it on his face and the backs of his hands. This would serve to dull the shine of his face. This being a scouting trip, he took no weapons but his knife.

That night he located the bandit's camp and sat a few hundred yards away watching. He could hear their voices but could not make out their words. He would take his time and learn their routine. When the time was right, he would strike, but for now he would bide his time and watch.

The next days were spent observing the outlaws and find-ing ways to creep closer. Each night before returning to his camp, he would slither closer and closer to their camp. When they moved their camp, he followed, and when they stopped, he would resume his reconnaissance. He slipped noiselessly among their horses. By the end of the first week they were accus-tomed to his coming and going by night and ignored his move-ments. Inch by inch he slid forward just outside the firelight.

It was too large a group to tackle head on, so he had to find some way to separate them. While he gave this thought, he listened to their conversations and learned the names of those he did not know. He also learned some of the personalities of those following Jacobs.

Wolfe, one of the ones who attacked his home, was spoken of as a gunfighter. He had killed men in gunfights and even Jacobs was careful around him. The reason he was not in charge was he simply did not want the responsibility of leadership. Jacobs, with a few exceptions, usually planned well. Bug-eyed Keegan was among them too. Ever looking for the boss's favor. Abbott was there as well, the man who had used the whip. Smith and Davis were newcomers as were the rest.

Almost three weeks of watching and waiting was growing tiresome, but Jim had learned patience. It had been almost four years since his family had been brutally slaughtered. A little more time to pick the right moment would not matter. Tonight he was within five yards of them.

"We're getting low on whiskey!" moaned Demming, one of the new gang members.

"Yeah, and I ain't seen a woman in two months neither," whined Abbott. "When we getting outta this wilderness and back to where we can enjoy ourselves?"

Wolfe laughed. "You boys are forgetting, we can't go just ride into a lot of places around here. Give Jacobs his due. He's got something in the works. After that I'm betting we can all go somewhere warmer and enjoy plenty of whiskey and women."

"We been waiting on something, and, if my calendar is right, it's time for us to make a good haul and then scatter."

"Ever hear of a town called Elk Horn?" Jacobs did not wait for an answer. "It ain't much of a place, but there's a bank there that handles a lot of cash money. You see, there's been some rich strikes in the area, and Elk Horn's where the dirt-muckers bring their dust to trade for cash. About now the bank should be flush, and with it being such a small town, we should have easy pickings."

Jacobs continued, "Tomorrow morning I'm sending Wolfe, Smith, and Davis on a little scouting mission. When they get back, we'll make the final plans. Any problems?" Nobody voiced any.

Wolfe smiled at the others he was playing cards with. "Well, boys, looks like luck is turning. I'll up my ante by twenty."

The last two men in the game folded and Wolfe raked in the pot. Then they all joined in the celebration finishing off what little liquor was left in camp. It was late before the outlaws decided to turn in, but Jim had his opportunity. He slipped back from the criminal contingent and trotted silently back to his own camp.

Lobo, would take two of the new gang members with him into town. They were to scout out the bank and local law enforcement. In two days they were to report back with their findings. The gang would finalize their plans then.

This was the opportunity Jim had been waiting for. He would travel ahead of the trio and pick his spot for the confrontation. Wolfe was reputed to be fast with a gun, but Jim had been practicing for hours every day since starting on this trail. Now his draw was almost flawless. His natural quickness of hand and eye had helped to make his own draw incredibly fast and he could call his shots with complete confidence. If he played his cards right, Wolfe would be the only one he would have to face.

Twenty-four

Riding out before dawn, Jim took a route that would keep him well out of view from the trail. He had seen a place that would fit his needs several miles from the outlaw camp and headed for it. Riding his mounts in relay, he arrived hours ahead of his quarry. That would give him plenty of time to set up and for his dust to settle.

One item that he had purchased during his last visit to town was a highly polished steel mirror. On a ridge overlooking the trail, Jim placed the mirror so that the sunlight reflecting from it would be visible from only one spot on the trail. He placed it behind a bush that looked like one a hidden gunman or watcher might use for cover. The movement of the branches in the breeze would cause the reflection to flicker rather than be a constant reflection.

He had already hidden his horses farther down the trail so that they would not be spotted nor give their position away to the outlaws horses. Now he was hidden close to the trail in a shallow depression that looked like there was not enough cover for a jackrabbit to hide in. He had learned from the Cheyenne how to remain motionless and hidden from an enemy even when in plain sight. The well-tanned leather of his clothing blended perfectly with the weathered grasses surrounding his hiding spot. Drawing both pistols, Jim placed them under his body and settled down to wait.

While Jim started his plan in motion, Wolfe and the other two outlaws lazed around camp until the sun was well into the sky before heading for the small town of Elk Horn. They were looking forward to spending the night in town and rode that way eagerly. Even so, they kept a watchful eye on the landscape around them.

The trio approached a tree dotted ridge to the west of the trail they paid close attention to the ridgeline. The area close to the trail was too sparse to hide anything but the ridge offered plenty of cover for a concealed gunman. A slight breeze ruffled the leaves of a scrub oak and the sun reflected off something metallic hidden behind the bush a hundred yards away. Their attention was completely focused on the slight flash of light from the ridge when the howl of a hungry wolf came from almost underfoot where an apparition rose from the dust with two drawn and cocked Colts.

The outlaws' horses went wild with panic and the unsuspecting riders were dumped unceremoniously into the dirt by their plunging mounts. When they arose from the ground, a dust-covered man with icy blue eyes confronted them, pistols pointed almost negligently in their direction.

"Mr. Wolfe is the only one I want. You two toss your guns aside. Wolfe, you have a choice. You can either toss your gun aside and come along peacefully, or you can try your luck. I don't much care which," Jim growled at the trio.

The other two outlaws looked to the man they called Lobo for direction, but it was Jim that gave it to them. "I said shuck them guns or I'll shoot you where you stand! It'll be two less highwaymen for the world to worry about, Mr. Smith and Mr. Davis."

"How'd you know our names?" demanded Mr. Smith.

"The same way that I knew where you would be today. I'm a shadow, only quieter at night. I could have spit into your coffee last night or your whiskey the night before. Mr. Davis, you should have played those three sixes last night. Lobo was bluffing with nothing but a queen."

Davis and Wolfe realized that Jim had somehow been close enough to see their cards as they played poker the night before. They also realized that he had been that close without them knowing or even suspecting. A chill ran up Davis's spine like the icy touch of the hand of Death. He very carefully tossed his pistol to the side.

Smith hesitated and began to raise his pistol casually. "I don't think the pup's got it in him."

Jim's left-hand Colt spouted flame and the slug ripped through the throat of the doubter. The soft tissue in the front of his throat did little to slow the bullet's progress, so it had sufficient force to smash the outlaw's vertebrae and sever his spinal cord. Eyes wide with shock, he fell to the ground like a puppet that had all of its strings suddenly cut. He was unable to do anything but drown in his own blood.

"Wolfe, it's your turn now. You can toss your gun aside and come along peacefully, or we can holster our weapons and see what happens. It's more chance than you gave my family."

Jeremiah Wolfe was smiling as he looked from Jim to the newly departed Mr. Smith and then up the ridge at the mirror. "Pretty slick," he said with a touch of admiration. "You pick an unlikely spot to hide and then distract us with that mirror in the likely spot for hiding. I presume that it was you that howled and not a for-real lobo. I expect that was partly to startle the horses and partly for Ole Lobo's sake." Looking at Smith he continued. "That one never was too smart." He shook his head and continued, "I don't think I've seen it done any slicker, but if the pup thinks he's grown long enough teeth to try me, who am I to refuse. One thing though, if you holster those pistols, there won't be any tricks you can pull. It'll just be you and me."

"No tricks," Jim stated flatly as he holstered both of his Colts. "I figured you wouldn't want to go peacefully to be hanged. Whenever you're ready."

Lobo was extremely confident. He had been through at least a half dozen gunfights and had come out on top every time. He knew he was fast and couldn't believe that Jim was giving him an even break. If the tables were turned, he sure wouldn't do the same.

"You've got guts, pup. I'll give you that, but it won't do you no good." As he stopped speaking, Jeremiah "Lobo" Wolfe's hand dropped to the butt of his gun. The move was smooth and practiced. He was smiling as his pistol began to clear leather and tilt toward his target. The smile was still on his face when he felt the impact of the .45 caliber slug from Jims' pistol smash through his breastbone to shatter his heart. It was still there as his eyes began to glaze over and his unfired pistol fell from his fingers. "You beat me, pup!" were the last words he spoke as he twisted and fell onto his side in the dust. The light of life had vanished from his eyes, and Lucifer welcomed one more to their eternal home in Hell.

Turning to Davis, Jim ordered him to take off his boots. "Pull the other two's off too and put them all in a pile and back up." The outlaw quickly obeyed.

Jim scooped up the boots and weapons before backing into the brush and disappearing. Davis didn't move for several minutes. He had never seen anyone come close to beating Lobo, and this dust-covered kid had not only given him an even break but had let the gunman make the first move.

He was still trying to decide what his next move should be when a voice drifted to him from somewhere out of sight. "I'll leave your horses and belongings a couple of miles up the trail toward town. Get them. Load your partners onto their horses and take them back to your camp. The walk will give you some time to think. Tell Jacobs that the bank is secure and James Harding sends his regards. Don't stay long in that camp if you want to live. I'll know if you follow my instructions."

The clatter of multiple horses' hooves could be heard heading down the trail from a different direction than Davis had thought the voice was coming from. He felt completely alone and helpless. Realizing exactly how vulnerable his position was, he started to follow the departing horses as quickly as his bare feet would carry him. As the sound of departing hooves faded away, panic began to set in and the outlaw began to run. Stumbling and falling, he ran as quickly as he could.

His feet were bruised and bleeding by the time he arrived where the outlaw's horses were tied. As promised, all of the belongings were there. There was a large note attached to the bridle of his horse. While he didn't read well, there were only two words on the note: "I'll know." The outlaw decided right then and there to follow all of Jim's instructions including the one about leaving Jacobs. A career change far from Montana seemed like a very good idea. He might even start using his real name again. Funny thing was his real name was the one his dead partner had been using, Smith.

Jim circled back to make sure that his instructions were being followed. He watched from cover as Davis loaded the bodies onto their horses and headed back toward the outlaw camp. When a coyote stopped in the middle of the trial and stared at him, Davis took it as an omen. Whether he was being watched by the man who had killed Wolfe or not, he was sure he was dead if he stayed with Jacobs.

Jim had circled around the camp to watch the effects of his message. Using the noise of the approaching Davis to mask his movements, he crept in close enough to see and hear what transpired. The fading light concealed any motion that might have been noticed.

"Hello the camp." Davis announced his approach. "It's Davis."

Curiosity drew the attention of the entire gang to the bodies bound across their saddles. Jacobs strode forward and lifted each of the dead men's heads by their hair so he could look at their faces. He knew who they were without looking, but he checked them just the same. Smith's head moved to an unnatural angle and the ugly hole in his throat dribbled blood down the saddle.

Visibly shaken, Jacobs asked, "What happened? You couldn't have gotten to town and back already."

"Boss, he caught us completely by surprise. We was riding to town and a flash of light caught our attention. When we turned toward it, there was the howling of a wolf and this feller just appeared from nowhere. The horses were so scared they pitched us all to the ground and run off."

Davis continued to give the narration, holding the interest of the entire camp. He seemed to remember the details completely and recalled it to his fellow gang members vividly. He shuddered slightly as he finished. "He plugged Smith in the throat and just let him drown in his own blood. Then he says to Lobo, 'You've got a choice. Toss your gun aside and come along peaceful or we can holster our guns and see what happens.'

194

"Lobo was good, so he just smiled and accepted the offer. This feller just holsters his Colts and waits. 'Whenever you're ready,' he says. You'd think with Lobo he'd of looked for some edge, but he don't. He just waits. He didn't even make his move until Wolfe had his hand on his gun. Then he just drags iron and drills Ole Lobo dead center. Lobo didn't even get a shot off. He barely even cleared leather."

Several gang members looked nervous. Some had seen Lobo in action, and the thought of this stranger waiting for him and giving him more than an even break before drilling him was mighty disconcerting.

Davis continued on. "Next he takes our boots, guns, and horses and takes them down the trail a piece and leaves them just like he said he would. He told me the walk would give me a chance to think and he suggested that I quit this outfit. He said to 'Tell Jacobs that James Harding sends his regards and that the bank in Elk Horn is secure.'"

Jacobs face blanched. Not only was this son of a Montana Ranger not dead, but he was hunting them down. He'd beaten Wolfe to the draw easily and had been close enough to their camp to actually see the cards in their hands without them knowing. It made a man wonder. It made matters even worse knowing how someone matching James's description had killed Gates and Seevers and had been seen in the area when Taggert had been killed.

Davis interrupted his thoughts. "I'm riding out, boss. Watching that Harding at work gave me the willies. You fellers can keep my cut from the last job."

Without waiting for a reply, he mounted and turned to ride out of camp. Having delivered his message, he saw no sense in taking his time following the rest of his instructions. He had no

desire to be around when that handy youngster caught up with
the rest of the gang.

Seeing one of his gang getting ready to abandon him,
Jacobs started to act. He drew his heavy Iver Johnson pistol
and pointed it at Davis's back. Before he could do more than
point it, a Cheyenne war arrow streaked from somewhere
in the darkness and pierced the gang leader's forearm. His
pistol clattered to the ground and everyone scattered for cover
except for the departing Davis. Nobody else tried to interfere
with the former gang member's departure.

The gang had lost all interest in sleep for the night. That
arrow had come from nowhere and had hit Jacobs's gun arm as
if drawn by magic. Some of the gang members were superstitious
and the recent happenings were making them nervous,
to say the least.

The next morning a note was found attached to a tree
encouraging those who had not been at the Lazy H to depart.
It was attached to a tree at the end of the picket line and had
been left without the horses making any fuss. The superstitious
in the group were even more shaken up and a couple of
them decided it was time to look for greener pastures. They
faded to the back of the pack as they pulled out and drifted off
into the brush when nobody was looking. And then there were
seven. Jacobs had lost half of his backers once again.

Jim picked up their trail the next day and followed at a
distance. He noted the places where a few had drifted off leaving
the main party weaker. Abbott, Keegan, and Jacobs were
the ones he wanted. The others he had very little interest in
other than how much they would interfere with his plans. He
would follow. He would bide his time and study his options,
at least for now. For now their guard was up.

They had argued about the Elk Horn job but decided against it thinking Jim would have warned the bank making it too risky for now. It was agreed to pick a few smaller targets. They could return for the big take another time. What they needed was eating and drinking money if Jacobs was to hold them together.

Twenty-five

The town of Bear Creek offered a bit of refuge, and perhaps they could gather some information there. If not they could resupply and move along picking up what they could along the way.

At Bear Creek station they picked up on a conversation regarding some recent strike in the Big Horns. They decided they would swing back toward the southeast. The Big Horns were open now and there was gold there. Gold for digging or for the taking. And the only law was what a man made for himself. They quickly made their purchases and rode out of town.

Jim pulled up in front of Bear Creek Station a full two hours after the Jacobs gang left town. The saloon was bustling, but Jim saw no faces he recognized. The town of Bear Creek was a sort of safe haven where outlaws could spend ill-gotten gains. Nobody asked questions. Nobody cared. Due to the type of town it was, sarsaparilla was not available, so Jim had coffee and helped himself to the lunch bar.

Having scanned the room on entering and not finding those he sought, Jim decided to try and gather some information. "I've been trying to catch up with some fellers I know," he said to the bartender. "I'm thinking they may have stopped in here on their way through." Jim then gave a quick description. "You wouldn't have happened to notice them would you?"

"Mister, you shouldn't oughta be asking questions around here. Nobody knows nothing and nobody's seen nobody. Were I you, I'd just let it ride in this town."

"Nobody'd help a man find some old acquaintances?" Before the barkeep could answer, a sandy-haired man who had heard Jim's first inquiry spoke up. "You heard him. Nobody knows nobody." The man's yellowed teeth were misaligned and formed a sneer. "What are you, some kind of law dog? We don't take kindly to them around here."

"I'm no lawman," Jim replied. "I'm just looking for some-one I know."

"If you're no law dog, then you're even worse, a bounty hunter!" The man was truculent and leading up to a killing. His holster was tied low on his right hip and he rested his hand on the butt of the Smith & Wesson forty-four it carried.

"I already told you, I'm not a lawman, and I'm certainly not a bounty hunter. My business with them is my business. It is of a personal nature. Let's just say I'm returning a favor."

"No, you're a scalp collector, a dog gone bounty hunter is what you are. That's what I say, and if you say different, then you're calling me a liar."

"Okay, you're a liar," Jim replied matter-of-factly.

The man's hand was already gripping the butt of his gun. He curled his thumb around the hammer and eased it back as the gun cleared leather. His finger was sliding into the trig-ger guard and his eyes danced with a killing fire. The barrel began to tilt away from his body when the shot sounded and the smell of burnt powder touched his nostrils.

"That's strange," he thought, and a second shot sounded. "I don't remember pulling the trigger." Then the fire faded from his eyes and he folded to the floor. He was right. He had not pulled the trigger.

Jim calmly punched the two spent cartridges from his right-hand Colt and reloaded. "If anyone knows where to take him, I'm sure his carcass is worth something."

"Sorry about the mess and the fuss," he said to the bartender. "I guess you were right. Nobody knows anything."

"Mister, do you know who you just killed? That was Bart Massey! You called him a liar to his face and gunned him without him firing a shot. I'd've never thought it could be done. He's got friends in town though, so was I you, I'd skedaddle. I'd probably head toward the Big Horns if I were you."

"Thanks for the coffee and the advice. I suppose a night under the sky won't kill me." Jim slipped out the batwing and swung aboard the roan as the undertaker arrived to collect the remains of Bart Massey.

Jim rode out of town to the north. He had not missed the directions given by the bartender, but he felt it best to misdirect anyone who might decide to follow him. He doubted the friends of the deceased would hunt very long or hard for him. Criminal enterprise rarely brings great loyalty. Criminals are criminals because they are self-centered and care little about others.

Jim was right. When Bart Massey's friends couldn't find Jim in town, they headed for Bear Creek Station and had a drink to Bart's memory. Then they promptly forgot about him. Jim gave him even less thought.

The next day Jim swung east for several miles before cutting back south searching for the trail of those he sought. Shortly before noon he crossed the trail of several shod horses. He held up to study them closely. He knew he was on their trail again. They were several hours ahead, but he was in no hurry.

Abbot swore as the sorrel stud he was riding started to favor his offside front foot. "Hold up," he hollered while pulling his horse to a stop. He slipped to the ground to check on his mount. "This nag's gone lame. I think he picked up a stone." The horse had indeed picked up a stone bruising the tender sole of his hoof. Abbott worked the stone free, but the horse still limped. To ride him now might injure him beyond healing.

"We'll ride on ahead and set up camp," Jacobs stated. "Then I'll send someone back for you with one of our horses. I heard there's a creek a few miles ahead, so somebody should be back for you just after dark or thereabouts. Just wait here and let that jughead take it easy and he'll be fine." Abbott didn't look happy, but he had no choice. He stayed put.

The afternoon sun was warm and Abbott dozed. There was nothing else for him to do unless he wanted to walk, and he hated to walk. He leaned back against a large rock and tipped his hat over his eyes.

"Hello, Abbott."

The voice shocked him awake, and he found himself looking up at the silhouette of a man sitting astride a strawberry roan with the sun behind him.

He shielded his eyes and squinted against the sun's glare. "Do I know you?" he growled.

"Maybe you do and maybe you don't, but I sure remember you." The man spoke evenly. "You used to use a black snake whip really good."

Abbott's face contorted slightly as realization came to him.

"What's the matter, Abbott? Didn't you get my regards?"

"Harding," the outlaw whispered.

"So you do remember me?" Jim said in mock surprise. "What's the matter, Abbott? You look like you've seen a ghost. Or maybe you aren't so tough when you're facing a man

who isn't tied down? I told you I'd come for you didn't I?'
Jim taunted. He had seen the sorrel picketed alone and had
scouted around before approaching. He knew Abbott was
alone but had no idea for how long.

"Stand up!" Jim ordered. "Then real carefully drop your
pistol in the dust, or try for it. Unless you are a lot faster than
Wolfe though, it won't do you any good."

The outlaw stood slowly. Very deliberately he drew his
pistol and tossed it aside. Sweat beaded on his face and he
licked his lips. "Ah, the boys'll be back soon," he tried to bluff.
It would be at least a couple hours before anyone came back,
if they did. He didn't think Jacobs would abandon him, but
stranger things had happened.

"Thanks, Abbott," Jim drawled. "You just told me what I
needed to know. They left you here. I can tell from your voice.
They aren't coming back, at least not for a while."

His bluff had backfired on him and now Abbott began to
panic. He turned to run, but before he had gone twenty yards,
Jim's roan overtook him and knocked him sprawling in the
grass. As he tried to rise, he felt his whip tied to his left hip.
Panic subsided and confidence took its place. He unfastened
the whip as he stood. Taking the whip stock in his right hand,
he let the fifteen feet black snake dangle at his side. He could
use the whip, at close range, faster than most men could use a
pistol and had cut the heads off rattlesnakes with this weapon.
He allowed himself to be herded back toward the rock, the
whip uncoiling behind him.

Jim swung down from the saddle and bent to retrieve
Abbott's sidearm. As Jim stooped to pick up the discarded
weapon, Abbott struck. There was a faint hiss in the air and
Jim felt a burning lash to his left shoulder, then the flow of
blood. He straightened and reached for his right-hand Colt.

Before he could bring it to bear, the whip cracked again and the gun was torn from his hand.

As the whip lashed forward again, Jim threw up his left arm to protect his neck and face. The tip of the whip could remove an eye or open the throat. Either one would mean the end for Mister James Harding. As it was, the braided leather strap tore his shirt and cut a gash in his forearm.

Already bleeding from two blows, Jim knew he would be cut to ribbons if he did not act. He could attempt to retreat, which most men would do, or he could attack. To attack would be unexpected and that was exactly what Jim decided to do.

As the whip flashed forward again, instead of trying to back away and avoid the blow, Jim stepped closer and threw his arm up wrapping the last few feet of the whip around it. He tried to jerk the weapon from Abbott's hand, but Abbott held tight and tugged in return.

Allowing himself to be pulled forward, Jim propelled himself feet first into Abbott's middle. A whoosh of air escaped him and he lost his grip on the whip stock. Abbott fell to the ground. Jim snatched up the whip stock and clubbed him in the side of the head knocking him out cold.

Abbott awoke to the sensation of the late afternoon sun on his back. He found himself secured to the rock he had been leaning against earlier as he napped. His shirt had been removed exposing his pale skin to the sunlight. A fly landed on his ear and he tried to shoo it away.

"Glad to see you with your eyes open," Jim said quietly. "I want you to see what's coming."

"What's coming?" whispered the bound man.

"Yes, what's coming," Jim put his face down next to Abbott's ear. "It's called justice. The Good Book says it like this: 'eye for eye, tooth for tooth, hand for hand, foot for foot, burning for burning, wound for wound, stripe for stripe.' It's in there, so it must be right."

He showed the quivering man the whip. "I'm not as good with this as you are, but I'll get by." Jim stepped back. At the crack of the whip, Abbott screamed in agony. An ugly red welt grew across the white of his back. Again the whip fell and the outlaw cried out. Blow after blow rained onto the exposed flesh, cutting and drawing blood. The man who had inflicted so much pain on Jim blubbered like a baby, begging for mercy. Blood flowed down his back and Jim stopped. It wasn't mercy that stopped him but a sense of wasted effort. While there were cuts and welts across Abbott's back, it was nothing compared to those he had inflicted on young James Harding those years before. There was no satisfaction, just a great feeling of contempt for this whining wretch before him.

"You're pathetic! You cry like a baby and beg for mercy. You make me sick. I'm taking your guns and turning your horse loose. Then I'll leave you."

"You're not going to kill me?" sobbed the beaten man.

"You aren't worth it, but just the same, don't tempt me." Jim's voice was a growl. "If I ever see you again, I'll consider myself tempted. Is that clear?"

Abbott simply watched what he could as Jim carried through with what he said he would do.

"You're not leaving me staked here, are you?" his voice was filled with fear.

"No," Jim said after a moment. "I'll cut you loose. But if you try anything, I'll stake you back out for sure. Now shut up while I send your horse on his way."

The sorrel was led off and given a slap on the rump to send it limping away. The bruised hoof would heel quickly without the weight of saddle and rider. Jim rode back and with a slash of his knife released Abbott's bonds. He took the lead rope of his packhorse and started off down the trail of the remaining men he hunted.

Unknown to either man, a pack of hungry wolves had been drawn to the sound of the horses. They had remained out of sight but watched what took place. The instinctive fear of man kept them back, but hunger kept them close. Now one of the humans was leaving and the horses were as well, but there was the smell of blood. Cautiously, watching Jim ride away, the wolves left their hiding place and glided forward.

It was growing late and Jacobs should be sending someone for him. Next time he had a chance he would kill James Harding, he promised himself.

Wolves normally will not attack a healthy adult human. They have a fear of man instilled in them by God at the time of the flood. But hunger and the scent of blood can override instinct.

Unaware of what was happening behind him, Jim rode forward on his quest. Twenty minutes down the trail he heard a horseman approaching at a cantor. Swinging quickly from the trail, Jim secreted himself in the brush to watch the rider approach. It was one of Jacobs's men and he was leading a spare horse. As the man rode past, Jim had to decide whether to follow him or go after his last two targets. He decided to continue on his original course.

Abbott became aware of the wolves as skulking shadows. For ten minutes they would stalk closer and then retreat at the smell of a human. They grew bolder, drawn by the smell of blood and fear. Without some type of weapon, Abbott was helpless, but the wolves did not know that, yet. He cast about for something with which to defend himself and his eyes settled on the whip, which lay where Jim had discarded it.

As the wolves grew bolder, Abbott raced at them cracking the whip and bellowing like a madman. They retreated then circled and came closer. There was noise, but noise wouldn't hurt them. Again he charged and again they retreated, but not as far this time.

The wolf pack circled, drawn ever closer by the blood they could clearly smell. The lash of the whip stung one of the wolves and they fell back again.

The pack tightened their cordon, and when next the whip cracked, one of the brutes caught the lash in its powerful jaws. Abbott could not free the whip, and rather than be dragged to the ground by the beast holding the whip end, he released his grip and turned to flee.

No man alive can outrun a hunting wolf. Within ten strides, sharp teeth clamped on his calf ripping muscle and tendon. Tumbling headlong onto the ground, Abbott did a somersault and landed face up staring into the eyes of the wolf his whip had marked. He tried to rise, but his leg would not support him, and the wolf lunged for his throat. Instinctively, he threw his arm up and was borne back to the ground, his arm mangled by strong canine teeth.

The struggle was brief. For less than a minute, Abbott held the wolf from him. The animal's hot breath stung his face. Others closed in tearing at his legs and sides. He felt hot all over. He never knew a wolf's breath was so hot. It felt like he was on fire and he cried out, "Oh, God in Heaven!"

"Your god, yes. In Heaven, no," said a voice. Then all was blackness and fire. The wolves were gone, but this was worse, far worse. "Welcome to Hell, my child," said the voice, then he was utterly alone.

Martin Trask rode onto the scene just a few minutes later. He hated wolves for some unknown reason and charged the pack firing as he raced toward them. At the time he had no idea what they were tearing at and didn't care. One wolf tumbled dead and the others scattered. Trask dropped another one before they reached the safety of the surrounding woods. Hungry or not they left the area in full retreat.

Trask cursed them and then laughed. "I bagged two of them before they got away." It was not until that point that he noticed the torn body of the man he was supposed to bring back to camp. "Abbott?" he said, hardly believing his eyes. Then he cursed the wolves again.

"How did they get to you?" he wondered out loud. For the first time he noticed that Abbott's horse was gone. A search of the area showed that all of his weapons were missing as well.

"Well, old son, there's nothing I can do for you now. I did do for a couple of them that got you, but danged if that will give you much comfort." He searched Abbott's pockets and took everything of value. "You won't be needing this anymore." He stated ruefully before mounting and heading back toward camp. Jacobs wouldn't like this at all.

Jim swung off the trail a mile from the camp and waited for Trask to return. He would wait to see what effect Abbott's report would have. When Trask returned, he led a riderless horse. Jim crept nearer to listen to what was said.

"It was wolves that got him," Trask repeated. "His horse and guns were gone. I hate the things, so I killed a couple before I even knew what they were squabbling over. It was Abbott. Funny thing though, as much as I hate them things, I've never known them to attack a healthy grown man. And where were his guns and his horse?"

All of the men around the fire looked nervous. They were thinking of the story of the "wolf howl" when Wolfe was killed in the not too distant past. Those who were not superstitious still wondered, what if he could talk to wolves and have them do his bidding. "We better not separate anymore," said Jacobs. "It seems that when we do someone dies."

Jim listened a little longer before slipping silently back to his horses to prepare a cold camp. He smiled to himself. It seemed they were all jumping at shadows and some thought he might have some supernatural ability to communicate with wolves. Maybe he could play on that some. Had he listened a few more minutes he may have changed his plans to counter theirs.

The outlaw camp was a dry camp that night. That is to say, there was no alcohol consumed. Guards were posted, and before daylight they were moving toward the Black Hills at a rapid clip. They took no pains to hide their trail, but they had not done so all along. Now there was purpose to this apparent negligence.

Passing through a narrow ravine, they headed toward a grove of trees a quarter of a mile from the mouth of the defile. The trail was clear and did not alter course. Then they stealthily swung back to the opening.

While in the ravine their pursuer would naturally be cautious. When leaving the ravine, his attention would be on the wood line before him. When he was a hundred yards out on the flat, they would open fire on him from the cliffs, surrounding the mouth of the ravine. The only drawback would be if he was able to make it to the wood line. To that end, two men were to shoot the horses after the first shot was fired.

Jim rode through the crack with every sense alert. If he were trapped in here, it would be tough sledding to get out alive. Every sense was alert. His eyes scanned the walls and rock outcroppings, but he spotted nothing. The hair on the back of his neck prickled, but there was no sign of danger.

Finally the passageway opened and he blew out his breath in a sigh. He halted for a moment and patted the roan's neck."I had a bad feeling about that place, but I guess it was just the jitters." The trail laid clear ahead and he moved out slowly scanning the woods to his front. "If they set up there for an ambush, we'll have to hightail it back up that ravine."

Jim turned to check for the smoothest route just in case and saw someone rise from cover on the canyon wall. A slug from a Henry rifle smashed through his shoulder. As he felt himself twisted in the saddle, other rifles joined in. The pinto went down in a heap and a bullet tore through Jim's thigh on its way into the torso of the roan. His mount reared and spun. Another slug struck the pommel of his saddle and tore a gash in his side. Then Jim fell from the saddle and the roan's knees buckled. The valiant steed toppled on his side, kicked a few times then lay still.

Jim knew he had been hit and hit hard. When the roan fell and was still, he rolled close to the horse for shelter until the fusillade ended. He had to stay conscious. He had to think. He had to...

Twenty-six

He awoke to the sun beating down on him from directly overhead. A shadow crossed his face and he opened his eyes. The shadow passed again joined by another. "Why don't the shadows stay still?" he thought. Then he realized they were vultures. The carrion eaters were gliding lower and lower looking forward to this bonanza of food. Since nothing had moved for almost two hours, the scavengers were sure the three animals below would soon fill their crops to capacity.

It was this same lack of movement that convinced Jim's attackers that he was indeed dead. None wanted to get close, but they could all see the blood clear enough. After the first brief movement, the man they had ambushed was still. After watching for some time, they circled around again and continued on their journey without another glance.

Jim struggled to prop himself against his dead horse. There was water in the canteen and he needed water badly. He struggled with the stopper and almost blacked out again before getting a few swallows down his parched throat. He managed a second drink then recapped the canteen. While trying to assess his wounds, he blacked out again.

There was a fire burning and people moving about when he came to again. It was evening. At least he thought it was, but there was something between him and the stars. He knew what it was but could not make his mind comprehend. He attempted to sit up, which solicited a groan from his injured body.

"Hey there," said a gruff voice. "I just got you stitched up and plugged up. Lay still. I don't like to see my work all undone without it being a new bullet hole."

"Be still," continued the voice more gently. "I'll get you something to drink." A burly man with a thick black beard sat beside him holding a dipper of water. "Take a few swallows at a time. There's plenty, so no need to guzzle it down like rot gut."

After Jim had drank a dipper of water, he lay back. A tent! It came to him. He was in a tent. The man sitting beside him was wearing a blue uniform. *How do you like that*, he thought. *Just in the nick of time the cavalry arrives.*

"We were just about sure the buzzards was right when we found you. Our scouts saw them blasted things circling and trotted ahead and found you. A little bit longer and you'd have been worm food, but them boys know a little about wounds. They patched you up until we arrived.

"You must carry some lucky charm or something because you was hit four times and not a bone hit, but your hip and the bullet deflected off it. You lost blood, but some good meat and plenty of water and you should be right as rain. That and some rest, of course, providing there's no infection."

"Water," Jim croaked.

The cavalryman scooped another dipper of water from the water bucket and held it for Jim to drink. Jim drifted back to sleep. His sleep was haunted by dreams of wolves and gunfire. A girl with an angelic face surrounded by the glow of the sun beckoned him, but he turned aside. Then he was fighting and shooting and falling. He came awake bathed in sweat. In his thrashing he had started his side bleeding again. It was only a trickle, but he pressed his hand to it to staunch the flow.

The bearded man was beside him again. "You was a little feverish, but I think that's over. Course now I need to plug that hole in your side again." It only took a minute for the cavalry doctor to stop the bleeding again. "This ain't the first time you been shot up, young man. My expert opinion is for you to stop getting shot otherwise you may not make it to a ripe old age. Now get some sleep."

After another dipper of water, Jim tried to sleep again. This time the dreams were more peaceful. He awoke to reveille and the need to attend to nature. He was extremely weak and sore but determined to stand on his feet rather than use the chamber pot that was offered by the doctor.

"Suit yourself, but if you fall down and bleed to death, don't come crying to me."

The wound in his thigh made walking more hobbling than walking, but he made the nearest tree and relieved himself. He returned to the cot he had been occupying and collapsed exhausted by the effort.

"Well, I see you didn't bleed to death out there. That's a good thing. Doctor Carmichael, that's me, hates to fix a patient up just to have them die of stupidity. Next time take the crutch to help with the leg. Now let's get some food into you."

Jim spent the next seven weeks recovering under the supervision of the Army Medical Corps. By that time he was recovered enough to sit in a saddle. He was still very weak, but his strength was returning day by day. The fourth bullet had torn a gouge out of his right side. He didn't remember receiving that wound at all.

He rode out of Camp Custer astride a long-legged buckskin. The time spent recuperating would make Jacobs feel certain of Jim's death. Jim wanted to shake that certainty. He spread the word that he was alive and that he was hunting Jacobs.

Word on the "prairie telegraph" traveled quickly. Within ten days Trask had heard word of this. He passed word to the others in the gang and word reached Jacobs that day. The men stood together at a bar in some no-name town.

"He's not human," Trask stated. "It's Jacobs he wants. I'm hauling my freight."

"We been together a long while, but I'm disappearing." The bug-eyed Keegan finished his drink and left the bar.

Jacobs found himself alone. His gang had dispersed like fog under a warm sun. A sudden terror twisted his gut like a fist. "It just can't be," he muttered to himself. "He's been left for dead at least three times. It can't be him."

"You all right, mister?" the bartender asked. "You're talking to yourself."

Jacobs glanced up absently. "Oh, fine. I just know he's a ghost. Gotta be. Or maybe a demon from Hell. Give me a drink." Jacobs' hand trembled as he quaffed the liquor. He laughed nervously, then he fled the bar.

⤺ Twenty-seven ⤻

rask was standing at the bar of the Gold Nugget when a
stranger walked in. The stranger walked to the bar beside
him and asked for coffee. Maybe five foot seven inches
tall, the stranger was in his early twenties. He smiled like he
knew some deep dark secret. That made Trask nervous as did
the idea that this man was vaguely familiar.

"Hello, Trask," greeted the stranger. "How's Jacobs?"
The blue eyes were hard and contemptuous. Trask blanched.
"I don't know what you mean, stranger. Who are you? Do I
know you?" stammered the outlaw.

"You should keep better company, and next time you try
to kill a man, look him in the eye. Don't shoot from the rocks
and cliffs. And by the way, you do know what I'm talking
about. I'll give you one more chance to clear your memory.
You can remember or you can forget everything above ground.
So, Mister Martin Trask, what's it to be?"

"You're Harding aren't you?" The voice was barely a
whisper.

"Yep, now last chance, where's Jacobs?" The ice-blue
eyes bore holes into Trask. He tried to hold them and stare
Jim down, but it was no use. Averting his eyes he said, "I'm

not sure. We left him in some little no-name town about sixty miles west of here."

"See now, that wasn't so bad. They do say confession is good for the soul." Jim dropped the money on the bar for the coffee and slipped out the door like a ghost.

Jim stepped through the batwings of the bar in the town with no name. He made no pretense of being covert. He walked to the bar and asked for coffee. "Who knows where I can find Jacobs?" The question stopped conversation and heads swiveled his way.

"Who wants to know?"asked a slightly intoxicated individual.

"Why, I do of course. Now could you point me in his direction?"

The man stood to face Jim. "And just who are you?" he demanded.

"I wouldn't push it, Shorty," one of his friends stated.

"Shut up, Barney," he said over his shoulder. "Now again, just who are you? And what is Jacobs to you?" he said to Jim.

"I am my father's son, and Barney gave good advice. Now do they call you Shorty because of your stature or your brain power?"

It took a moment for the question to register. "Why you! You can't call me stupid and get away with it!" He reached for his gun.

Shorty was also short on speed. The bullet from Jim's left-hand Colt passed through his upper arm and his gun thudded into the sawdust on the floor. Jim's draw had been so casual that he was able to take the time to not kill Shorty.

"I told you, Shorty," said Barney. Then to Jim he said, "I take it you're Jim Harding. Jacobs was here a few days back with several other hard cases. They pretty much left him by himself. He rode out to the south two days ago. Hot footing down the trail like Lucifer himself was after him."

"Not Lucifer, but judgment sure enough. I do plan to help him meet Satan when I catch up to him though. Thanks for the information." Jim tossed a coin on the bar. "Sorry about the mess."

"Shorty, you better get that arm patched up before you bleed to death."

Jim left the bar and rode south. Two days head start. If he rode steady and did not rest, he could make that time up. He would have to swap horses, but that didn't bother him. A horse was a horse.

The trail was easy to follow. Played out horses were left and tales of a man, crazy with fear, blazed a clear trail. Jim continued his relentless pursuit. He rode steadily and didn't exhaust his mounts. Each time he stopped to swap horses or ask questions, he found he was gradually gaining. From a two-day lead to one of several hours.

He made a trade for a high stepping horse with a stubborn eye. The horse cost him thirty dollars to boot, along with the weary Appaloosa he was riding. But when he swung astride, he knew he had made a good trade.

"That fella you mentioned was here about two hours ago. I almost refused him a horse after seeing the condition of the one he rode in. Still not sure if we'll have to put it down or not. But he paid top dollar for one of the horses that just wasn't the best. You must be what he's running from." The man looked carefully at Jim's head. "Nope, didn't think I'd see any."

Jim looked puzzled.

Laughing, the man said, "Horns, the feller said you was the Devil or a ghost, so I thought I'd look for your horns."

Jim stood staring for a few seconds then laughed. "Nope, no horns on my head. As far as being a ghost, he's had a few tries at making me one. Much obliged."

Jim swung aboard and turned the horse down the trail. He set off at a lope then slowed to a trot after a few miles. The horse loved to travel and was almost impatient when his pace was slowed to a trot.

Alternating between the lope and the trot, Jim steadily gained on his quarry. Before too many hours, he spotted a dust plume several miles ahead. He stepped the pace up slightly.

The hours passed and the gap between him and the dust ahead steadily shrank. Jim slowed his mount again. Hours of steady travel were beginning to have an effect on even this magnificent animal. He slowed to a walk then dismounted to give the horse a rest.

"We're gaining horse. Not too many more miles and we can stop." Jim loosened the saddle and lifted it to allow some air to cool the horse's back. Then he fed him a hat full of grain and allowed him to drink from a small stream. He walked the horse for twenty minutes before tightening the cinch and climbing back aboard.

The short reprieve gave new life to the tired horse and he was eager to move. The dust plume grew steadily larger, and before long Jim could make out the figure of a horse and rider. Jim also noticed a collection of buildings toward which his harried foe headed. Jim calculated he would get to the town within a half hour of Jacobs's arrival. He could push his horse harder, but he refused to ride the horse to death just to catch Jacobs thirty minutes sooner. Let Jacobs sweat.

His quest, for he believed it to be just that, had lasted more than three years and was now drawing to an end. He had lost the trail more than once only to pick it up again with some information about a robbery or a description that matched Jacobs or his followers. There were only two left now and one of them was close at hand. The other had disappeared and was probably already dead.

He had spent countless dollars and thousands of hours hunting for his quarry. That wasn't counting the horses he had left by the wayside or the relationships he had never developed or discarded because they would interrupt his hunt. Only his family ranch remained.

Only a few more miles would bring him face-to-face with the man who, in his eyes, epitomized evil.

Twenty-eight

L ooking over his shoulder was how he lived now. Fear had crept into his soul, and he lived in that icy pre-death grave of dread. He had seen all of his confederates from the original raid on the Lazy H either killed or, in the case of Keegan, sneak away to hide in obscurity. He was alone now and just ahead of someone who had sworn to see them all dead for their crimes against his family. His hunter had accounted for all but one of them and had also cut a swathe through his new recruits every time their numbers grew. The new men weren't his real targets, so they were spared, on occasion, as long as they left at his command.

Ahead a town loomed, and he drove his lathered mount down the main street toward what, he didn't know. The staggering steel dust gelding collapsed in a heap before a large white building near the center of town. The rider rose and stumbled through the doors into the cool, almost empty interior of the Saddlestring Church. The horse struggled to its feet, head drooping and sides heaving for breath. The man pulled the heavy doors closed behind himself, began searching about for someplace to hide. The building's only other occupant rose from his knees near the altar and approached the fear-crazed outlaw.

"You look like the Devil himself is on your tail. What're you running from?" His calm attitude was in stark contrast to that of the man he faced.

"The Devil ain't nearly as relentless. He's been hunting me for over three years. I thought he'd been killed more than once and then he just appears again. He ain't human. He's a devil or a demon or a ghost or something." The man's eyes were darted from shadow to shadow. They were bloodshot and his voice cracked.

"Well, while I do believe that there are devils and demons, I don't believe your hunter is one. They usually stay hidden in the shadows."

"He killed the rest of them and now he's after me. You gotta hide me. He won't stop."

"What did you do to him?"

"Nothing!" Jacobs lied. "He just keeps coming." His voice shuddered when he spoke and the middle-aged man took pity on him, or maybe he just didn't want to witness the inevitable. The quivering man peered frantically out the front windows. He held his pistol in a trembling fist and he shook like a willow in a windstorm.

"You go out the back and take that old brown mare out there. She's old but reliable. Remember though, God knows what you're really running from. Unless you turn it over to Him, you will see real devils and demons. I'll talk to your hunter when he gets here."

The outlaw didn't waste time but headed out the rear door of the church without even a thank-you and climbed aboard an old brown mare. He rode from town toward the empty plains to the west whipping the horse into a gallop.

Another man entered the church. "Well, Preacher, what kind of mischief have you gotten into now? I saw that man ride off on your mare, and I don't think he could have taken her without your permission."

"Pastor Henry, how good to see you. I was hoping that you'd be here. I think I just postponed the inevitable, but I hope to stop murder from being done."

"Murder?"

"That feller that just rode off on that old mare of mine has someone on his trail. He wasn't honest with me about why, so I think his pursuer is the one that needs stopped for his own sake, not that other feller's."

"I don't follow you."

"I think he wronged his hunter in some horrible way. I'm more worried that whoever is tracking him will destroy their life in the taking of his. While I was praying here in your church, I just kinda got the feeling that I was gonna be doing some intervening today." Both men chuckled as they thought of what Preacher's "intervening" sometimes consisted of. Gunfight, fistfight, or knife fight, Preacher had few peers, and he could quote the Scriptures while whipping his opponent in any of them. (Usually the Old Testament.)

The men talked for several minutes while checking over the abandoned mount. Preacher noticed a plume of dust rising in the east and the two watched as they cooled down the steel dust. It gradually grew until both men could distinguish a single rider. Unlike the earlier man who entered town, he rode toward them at a gentle lope. Ten minutes later the rider pulled up in front of them. His horse was gaunt from travel but was under no duress.

The rider spotted the steel dust tied to the hitching rail and dismounted to check its condition. While he wouldn't hesitate to kill the former rider, the horse was innocent in his eyes. He could also determine how far ahead of him his prey was. He approached the horse warily, keeping his eyes on the surrounding buildings while speaking to it softly. He noted the scrapes on the animal's legs and shoulders and gingerly checked them by touch. His eyes hardened to icy blue daggers as he thought of how poorly the horse had been treated. The rifle was still in the scabbard and the stock had been smashed when the horse collapsed onto it.

"The feller that was ridin' him is gone. I already checked this big guy over before I tied him here. He's fine."

The newcomer turned to the speaker. "You say he's already gone? Which way did he ride out, and what was he riding?"

"Don't know for sure, but I'd say he headed to the west seeing as how you was coming from the east. He's riding my old mare, so I'd take it kindly if you'd leave him be. I hate to think of Ole Molly being ridden to death like that gelding nearly was." Preacher had approached to within a step or two of Jim. "Let it drop. He'll get his. His kind always does in the end."

"He slaughtered my family. You're right, he surely will get his as soon as I catch up to him."

"Not what I meant," replied the man called Preacher. "Why don't you take some time to think about it? Like I said, I don't want my Ole Molly gettin' ridden to death."

"Preacher, is this the man who is hunting the guy that took Molly?" Pastor Henry posed the question.

"I believe so."

"Well, Preacher, I appreciate the fact that you care about your mare, but I'm riding out after him now. There's nothing to think about."

Preacher had been giving some thought to the man he was facing. He had come up with a name. He had traveled the region enough to know the story. His family killed by outlaws, young James Harding had set out to make them pay and had done so thus far. Preacher had seen too many young men either destroy their lives or lose them in just such a quest. He was afraid that this one would destroy his.

"I didn't know your ma, or your pa or your sister, but I knew of him by reputation. I don't think they'd like what you're doing. I reckon I gotta stop you, Jim."

Jim had taken in the fact that Preacher was unarmed and appeared to be in his late forties or early fifties. He didn't think this "old" man could stop him. "Not today," he said. For emphasis he reached for his right-hand Colt.

Before he could draw the weapon, he found his wrist wrapped in a grip like the jaws of a bear trap. His move had been anticipated and countered. Unable to finish his draw or to pull his hand free from the grip, he abandoned his draw. Jim swung his left fist toward the jaw of the man who held his right wrist in a viselike grip. The punch was brushed aside and the elder man wrapped his right arm around the shoulders of his young assailant and threw him over his hip to the ground like a sack of grain. Shocked and stunned, Jim looked up in surprise at Preacher. This middle-aged man had pitched him to the ground like a rag doll and stood above him smiling.

With his face turning red, Jim bounded to his feet in an attempt to continue the confrontation. His blows were deftly blocked or evaded. Preacher pushed aside a right-hand blow with his own right. Gripping the wrist, he pulled the younger man past him and stepped behind him. Shoving forward on Jim's elbow with his left hand, he tripped the younger man forcing him helplessly to the ground. Placing his left knee in the center of the fallen man's back, he pinned him face down in the dust.

"I know you been through a lot, and losing your family to a gang of outlaws clouds your judgment, but you can't let that draw you into being one of them. You was set to draw on an unarmed man to keep up your hate. Now let's talk, and when we're done, if you still want to throw your life away by killing a man, I won't stop you."

Jim was completely at Preacher's mercy and knew it. "Fair enough. I've been hunting him for years. Ten more minutes won't make any difference."

Preacher rose to his feet and stepped back to watch Jim rise. "Most folks call me Preacher. Let's go have that talk."

Preacher led the way into the cool dark interior of the church. Motioning Jim to one of the hard pews in the front row, Preacher turned his back on him and walked toward the pulpit. He gazed up at the cross mounted on the wall gathering his thoughts.

"You know what that thing means, boy?" He motioned to the wooden symbol of Christianity. Jim just stared. "It means that we ain't got no right to take the law into our own hands. You see, God done made somebody pay for it all already. That's what that cross means. The man that done it has far more reason to take care of that man you been hunting than you ever will, and instead He paid the price for his crime too. He suffered even more than you for what that feller did."

"What do you mean? It wasn't his family they butchered! It was mine!" His words rang hollow in his own ears.

"You see, that's where you're wrong. It was his family, and they was killed by members of his own family. He made us all in His image, so we're all kind of like family, and now it grieves Him to have us killing each other for revenge or greed or just 'cause we're mad. He can handle vengeance Hisself when and how he chooses. Killing someone while defending yourself or someone else or during war is one thing, but hunting them down without mercy like some animal is something altogether different. He told them that accused the woman caught in adultery that they could go ahead and stone her to death if any of them was without sin. Nobody threw a stone. If you're perfect and never in your entire life did anything wrong, go ahead and hunt him down like a dog. If not, maybe you should think about what this is doing to you. You're so ate up with hatred you can't see straight. Keep it up and your soul will be as black as theirs."

Jim gazed from the cross to the one called Preacher and back. He thought about all that he had tossed aside over the past years and what a horrible price he had paid for his hatred. He had no real friends. His business partner was just that and no more. Revenge had consumed him leaving him empty inside. He knew that when this quest for revenge was over he had nothing left. He was hollow inside and his hatred had filled that emptiness crowding out anything else. He knew that at times he had killed with very little thought and even less remorse.

"How do I let it go?" he whispered. "He was the one that led the raid. He's the one that...," he hesitated.

"Much as we hate it, Jesus died for him too. It's up to Him to decide what happens, maybe Hell, maybe redemption. Who knows? What you need to do is simple. It ain't necessarily easy, but it's simple. Ask Christ to forgive you for what you been doing and leave the rest to Him and the law."

James knew that what this man was saying was the truth, but it didn't make things easier. He had let his hatred eat at him for so long that it was like an old friend. He had nurtured it while he was recovering and let it give him direction in his grief, and now he had to put it away? He felt entitled to his hate. To him it was like a bottle to the drunk.

"How?"

Preacher pulled an old worn book from his pocket. The cover was heavy dark leather and the title was faded and illegible. The pages were dog-eared and yellowed from age and years of use. The binding was broken and some of the pages had come loose but were tucked back into their respective places. Preacher had memorized almost every page. His weathered hands caressed the cover like a parent caressing the face of a beloved child.

"It's all in here," he breathed. "You heard the Scriptures before ain't you? I reckon your ma read them to you even if your pa didn't."

"Yeah, Ma read them to us every night before dinner, and Pa prayed over us every night. He didn't realize it, but Rachael and I knew. That's just one more reason that Jacobs needs to pay. They say 'an eye for an eye,' don't they?"

"Sure they do, but that's dealing with the law, not revenge. They also say, 'Vengeance is mine I will repay saith the Lord.' Maybe he figured he could take care of it better than any of us could, so he wanted us to leave it to him. He told us to pray for our enemies. I don't think he meant for us to pray for them to succeed in doing wrong but that they would get right with Him. He doesn't want us to destroy ourselves because of our anger with them that did us wrong. Don't you think God's able to devise a more fitting end to that Jacobs feller than you are? All you can do is kill him. God can give him over to his nightmares for eternity. The funny thing is, according to God's law, we all deserve death and Hell, not just the ones like them that killed your folks."

"What can I do? What do I have to do?" Jim's face was contorted with confusion and inner pain. Warm tears slowly dribbled down his face as he remembered his mother's admonitions to forgive. They were the first tears to flow from his eyes since the death of his family. His father had taught him to care for others and to be willing to help. Even he, tough and capable as he was, had taught tenderness to his children. That was something that Jim had blocked out for the past few years, remembering only the anger and hatred.

"First you gotta confess that you can't do it on your own. He already knows that, but he wants you to admit it. After that you have to ask yourself what's the right thing to do. What would God want you to do?"

Jim knew that he was being told the truth. In a corner of his ever-darkening heart, a sliver of light began to grow. The teachings of Christ that his mother had insisted on had not been completely driven out and were now resurfacing. For the first time since the death of his family, he bowed to pray in earnest. The next several hours were spent in prayer and discussion with Preacher. They read passages from the weathered Bible dealing with loss and hope. At the end of their hours-long talk, Jim bowed to pray and even managed to turn his hatred over to God for his justice.

~∾ Twenty-nine ∾~

e rode out of town to the west at a gallop. The old mare was slower than the gelding he had nearly ridden to death, but she was fresh and his pursuer was riding the same mount that he had started the pursuit with. She should be able to keep him safely ahead of pursuit until he could acquire a new horse. His fear began to abate as the town disappeared in the distance.

He had lost him again. He was miles from town and Jim Harding would be hard-pressed to follow him now. Smiling slightly to himself, he glanced over his shoulder. To his dismay, he thought he could see a dust plume in the distance following him and pushed Molly a little harder. The dust cloud seemed to be growing closer and he pushed his mount just a little more. How could his pursuer possibly be gaining on him? He should be miles away and falling farther behind. Instead, when he sped up, so did the dust. Fear began to grow in his heart once again.

Molly began to falter, and Jacobs had to slow down or risk killing her. He couldn't risk being left afoot in the wilderness. Giving thought to his situation, he began to formulate a plan. He reached to the rifle boot only to realize that he had left his broken rifle in town along with his fallen mount. Panic started to spread. He looked over his shoulder again.

Dust sprang up and danced a few seconds before settling back down and quickly springing up hundreds of yards farther to the west. The dust clouds looked to be following the same trail that was being followed by the fleeing outlaw. The small dust devils fed his superstitious fears causing him to see what wasn't there, or maybe the demons really were there nipping at his heals.

A dust devil kicked up behind Jacobs and he was sure that he saw a horseman in the shimmering waves. Drawing his pistol, he fired a shot in the general direction of the apparition. The whirlwind vanished as Jacobs crested a small ridge. He had been riding into the sun and it now began to set and dusk started to envelope the landscape. His fear grew, as did the darkness. He found a small depression with dense brush surrounding it and decided to try and hide from his hunter.

Unable to sleep, the terror-filled criminal watched through the night. Hearing a small sound near the outer edge of the brush, Jacobs fired a shot. The scurrying of some small rodent drew another shot and so it went during the hours of darkness. Every sound drew fire and panic grew as the night wore on. Firing at the smallest of sounds and reloading when his revolver was empty, Jacobs stripped all of his ammunition from his belt. Shortly before dawn, Molly pulled loose from where she had been tethered and wandered away leaving her rider stranded.

The sun slowly crept over the eastern horizon. As the last vestiges of night were swept from the sky, Jacobs fired his last cartridge at a mirage that he thought was a man riding toward him. Realizing he was out of ammunition, Jacobs threw his empty pistol at a slight movement that he detected and fled from the depression in panic. He left his knife and cartridge belt lying in the depression in his flight from the imagined enemy.

The boots that he wore were not made for running in, but he tried nonetheless. Fleeing to the west, he broke the heel of his right boot and stumbled into a huge tumbleweed tearing large furrows in his sunburned skin. He stopped long enough to pull his boots from his feet and throw them into the brush. With his boots off he could travel faster until his feet began to bleed through his dirty socks.

He continued to weave his way to the west watching over his shoulder for the pursuit he felt but could not see. His water skin was on the saddle of the departed Molly and the sun began to drain him of moisture. "It sure is hot," he thought out loud. Sweat streamed down his face leaving trails in the dust that covered it. The salty liquid burned like tiny fires were being lit on his face and arms where the tumbleweed had torn the skin. Rivulets of muddy sweat ran into his eyes distorting his vision. Trying to rub the grit from his eyes only served to scratch them all the more.

Stumbling to the west, he continued to watch over his shoulder causing him to miss seeing an abandoned prairie dog hole. His foot crashed through the roof of the burrow previously occupied by the small rodent. Its current resident took exception to the intrusion and the small prairie rattle-snake struck quickly at the unprotected foot, injecting a small amount of venom into the offending appendage.

The snake was small, so the venom was far from suffi-cient to kill Jacobs by itself, but it was more than enough to cause his foot to swell and become stuck in the rocky opening. The snake decided that if the intruder would not leave then he would and crawled out the back entrance to the burrow.

Pulling frantically on his leg only caused his foot and ankle to swell more as the venom slowly worked its way through his body. Jacobs began to claw at the rocks and dirt surrounding the trap his foot had slipped into but to no avail. The only place not made of stone was the opening in which his foot was now wedged. Without tools there was no escape.

The poison from the snake mixed with the heat of the day began to wear on Jacobs's frazzled nerves. He began to hallucinate as dehydration and the venom worked on his mind. He saw, or thought he saw, a horseman approaching him and cried out. The dust devil collapsed and the "horseman" was gone. His mind continued to play its devilish game on him as the heat of the day pressed down on him like a physical force. When he could stand it no more, he reached for his pistol only to be reminded that he had discarded it along with his knife back where he had hidden during the night. He couldn't even end his suffering with a merciful bullet or a slash of his knife.

His tongue began to swell as he continued to dehydrate. His body stopped producing sweat to cool itself. When his tortured mind and body could take no more, he slipped into a catatonic stupor. Then he saw them coming. They were coming for him. Several riders or so he thought were coming straight for him. It was so hot. The heat increased as the riders drew nearer. It should be growing cooler, he thought, since it's growing darker, but as the darkness increased, so did the unbearable heat. There wasn't a drop of moisture to relieve his agonizing thirst.

As the blackness enveloped him and the insatiable heat surrounded him, he could finally discern the features of the riders. Blazing eyes and dark, ghoulish features stared down at him as the demons claimed their latest prize. His screams fell on deaf ears and his eternal soul received its just reward. Preacher had been right. He was seeing real demons now rather than those he imagined. They had finally caught up to him.

JIM STAYED IN Saddlestring for the next several days spending time with Preacher. He felt like a huge weight was being lifted from his shoulders. When the older man decided to leave town, he invited Jim to come with him. Preacher was heading in the general direction of Jim's Lazy H ranch and the two decided to travel together. The day that they rode out of town, Molly returned without her rider just in time to accompany the two as they left.

Thirty

It had been more than eight months since Jim's last departure from the Lazy H. Now he was returning, uncertain of his reception. He had abandoned them during round up when they needed him the most. Another time, in the aftermath of a deadly winter storm, he had left the work to fall onto the shoulders of his partner while he chased after his quest for revenge. There had been other times as well. True, it was part of their partnership agreement, but that did not make it right nor just.

There was yet another reason for Jim's apprehension. After meeting Preacher, the two had travelled together and made a stop in a small town along the way. The people there watched Jim as he rode toward a frame house on the edge of town. Some greeted him nervously while others watched curiously. One blond young woman watched with a mixture of smug satisfaction and open hostility. He had snubbed her during his last visit to this small burg and she resented him for it.

Jim dismounted in front of the house. He slowly stepped onto the veranda and tapped on the front door. He waited a few seconds then tapped again a bit louder.

His second knock was answered by a solid-looking man in his mid-forties. Jim doffed his hat. "May I speak with Madeline please, sir?" he asked softly.

"It has been too long, James," was the response. "I'm not sure she will want to see you."

"I understand, sir. I just wanted to…"

Drawn by the sound of someone speaking her name, Madeline appeared. "Who is it, Daddy?" she queried cheerfully. Seeing Jim she stared. Her mouth dropped open and a cloud seemed to appear over her face. She looked down at her shoes.

The corners of Jim's mouth twitched upward then down again as he tried to smile. "Madeline, I'd like to speak with you if I may." The light still played on her hair giving the halo effect he had noticed the first time he saw her.

"It has been a long time, James," she said quietly.

"Your father said you may not want to talk to me. I wouldn't blame you if you didn't. I treated you poorly."

"It's okay, Daddy. Maybe it's better this way." She looked at Jim.

Her father stepped aside. "I'll be right inside if you need me," he said to his daughter. He gave Jim a hard look before retreating to the interior of the house.

"You still look like an angel to me," Jim began."I know I rode out on you after all you did for me. I didn't give a thought to your feelings. I was wrong. I am very sorry. Can you forgive me?"

"You broke my heart, James Harding!" she replied, looking up into his eyes. "I saw all that was good in you and I gave you my heart. I loved you then and you refused my love. I was terribly hurt. Can you understand that? You gave me no reason I could understand and then left. I cried for days and waited hoping you would come back. But you didn't.

"Can I forgive you? I loved you, Jim, and I already forgave you. Eventually I gave up on you coming back. Patrick Swanson came courting. He's a good man, Jim. You would like him." She looked down as tears started to stream down her cheeks. "We are engaged to be married. He loves me and I love him. You were my first love, but he is my true love. I'm sorry."

She started to retreat into the house, but Jim's voice stopped her. "You have nothing to be sorry for," he stated quietly. His own voice was husky. "Patrick would be a fool not to love you. I was a fool. You were right to give your heart to someone who will cherish you. He's a lucky man." He kissed her gently on the forehead and walked to where Preacher waited with the horses. There was a slight mist in his eyes, and Preacher noticed the tears on Madeline's face before she retreated to the interior of her home.

"She met someone else. He's a good man," Jim said in a defeated tone. He swung astride his horse and thundered out of town at a gallop.

Preacher followed at a slower pace and caught up to Jim a little ways out of town, after Jim had slowed his mount to a walk.

"I was a fool, Preacher. She was sweet as sugar candy but I wanted revenge."

"Broken hearts mend, boy. As for being a fool, no man has the corner on that market." That was all that Preacher said on the subject.

That was four days ago. Now, as the two men rode into the ranch yard, a new wave of anxiety swept over Jim. Before he had pretty much come and gone as he chose. Looking back he could see he had used people as tools. He had let blind hatred thwart the friendship offered by the Daltons and others.

Until meeting Preacher, this would not have affected him. Now, with the changes taking place inside him, it left him uncertain and feeling small. Everything was different. The changes made him realize that others mattered and not just his ambitions.

Since the men were out working the range, the first person to spot Jim was Sarah. Her big brown eyes danced with merriment. A smiled played on her lips as if permanently affixed to her freckled face. Little Sarah wasn't as small as she had been the first time they met.

"Mommy, Mommy, Jim's home!" she shouted. Rufus came bounding out of the barn barking in greeting.

"Hi there, Sarah. You get prettier every time I see you." Jim smiled at her. "Sarah, I would like you to meet a friend of mine. This is Preacher. Preacher, this fair maiden is Sarah."

Dinah stepped out onto the porch. She had been busy getting the evening meal ready for Tom and the hands. The ranch was growing and could probably afford a cook, but Dinah enjoyed cooking for the hands. Everyone ate together in the dining room of the house. It made it feel like family.

"Hello, Dinah." Her brown eyes did not carry quite as much joy on seeing him. "It's good to be back. I'd like to introduce you to Preacher. Dinah, this is Preacher. Preacher, this is Dinah, Sarah's mother."

Preacher tipped his hat. "It's a pleasure to meet you, ma'am, although I'd of thought you was Sarah's sister, not her ma."

Dinah smiled at the compliment. "It's a pleasure to make your acquaintance as well, Preacher." Then she glared at Jim. "Why don't you put your horses up? Tom and the boys will be in shortly. Are you staying long this time, Jim?" Her question was tinged with anger. Her husband had to work out on the range far more than he would have had Jim been there to do his share. She did not like her husband sleeping under the stars rather than in her arms.

Jim looked down. "A good long while I hope."

He and Preacher strode to the barn and put their horses into some empty stalls. Sarah had followed them."Where did you go? Did you catch the bad men? Where did you meet Preacher? Are you a preacher, or is that your name? Why would your mommy name you Preacher?" The questions flowed without a breath or a chance to answer any of them.

"Slow down, little one." Preacher laughed. "I'm sure we'll answer most of your questions, but let us take care of these tired old ponies first. Molly here," he indicated his old mare. "She gets quite persnickety if I don't feed her when there's food close by. Besides, they been doing all the walking whilst we just sat atop them and enjoyed the ride. I figure it's only fair they eat first, since they did all the work."

He turned to Jim. "Is she always this curious?"

"Only on a slow day," Jim responded. "If you ask me, I think she's just getting warmed up." Both men laughed.

Sarah scowled at them for a moment then laughed herself. "Okay. I can wait, but you have to promise to tell me everything." She turned and skipped from the barn with Rufus bounding along after her.

Jim and Preacher carried their gear to the bunkhouse and got settled in to a couple empty bunks. Preacher hung his gun belt on a peg near the bunk he had selected. "Your pa built a nice place here. I'd say he built it to last."

Jim hung his head slightly, remembering all the hard work his father had put into building the ranch. He thought back to the day his family had been slaughtered and how his father's dream of a peaceful life was snuffed out. "Yeah. That's what he meant for it to do. That, and he wanted it to be a home. I don't know if it can ever be that for me. Maybe. I just don't know yet."

"Give yourself some time, James. It looks like it is becoming a home already for these folks. Maybe for you too. Maybe not. Don't try to hurry."

Several horses cantered into the yard amidst whoops and laughter. The barking of a dog added to the tumult and a child's squeal of delight could be heard above the din. "Daddy's home! Daddy's home!"

Jim and Preacher stepped from the bunkhouse and watched the homecoming from the shadows.

Tom bounded from his horse and scooped Sarah up in his arms swinging her around. "Oh my goodness, little one, you are getting big." He eyed her suspiciously. "Did you grow some since we rode out yesterday?"

"Daddy, you're silly. I can't grow that fast." Sarah giggled.

"Da Da Da." Little Tom scooted down the steps and toddled toward his father. His four front teeth showed in a wide smile. Tom picked him up and tossed him into the air to catch him and hug him close. Tom's face glowed with the joy of being a father.

"Sandy, would you mind taking care of my horse for me while I kiss the cook?" Tom turned to the puncher and tossed him the reins of his horse.

"Course not, boss, but remember we haven't eaten since before sunrise this morning, so don't you get carried away and distract the cook too long." The sandy-haired puncher laughed as he led the boss's mount to the barn to care for it.

Dinah was on the porch when the cavalcade arrived. She blushed slightly at the young cowhand's comment. Tom was affectionate, was not embarrassed to show his love for her or their children. If anyone didn't like it, he would say, "You should try it. Never miss the chance to let those you love know it. Tomorrow might be too late." That was his philosophy.

Tom strode toward the house with his name's sake perched on his shoulder and Sarah tagging along beside him. Dinah hurried down the steps and put her arms around her man. Holding Little Tom with one hand so he would not fall, Tom encircled Dinah with his free arm and kissed her soundly. "I sure do miss you when I'm gone," he said sincerely. Then he winked at her. "Do you think the cook might have a special dessert just for the boss?"

"Why, Thomas Dalton! Whatever do you mean?" She slapped him playfully with the towel in her hands. Then she smiled and winked back at him. "You'll just have to wait until later and see." She laughed. "Now go wash up or you might not even get dinner." She kissed him on his bristled check.

"Eww! You two are mushy," Sarah interjected. She wrinkled her nose.

Both parents laughed. "Someday I hope you find a man to be this mushy with," her mother said, still staring at her husband.

"Not for a good long time though!" her father said quickly.

Tom sat their son down and headed to the wash basin to attempt to clean some of the trail dust from his face and arms. He would take a trip down to the creek later to take a proper bath before bed, but for now this would have to do.

The hands cared for their mounts and then trooped to the bunkhouse to stow their gear and dust themselves off. "Howdy, boss." Sandy brought up the rear but was the first to greet Jim. He somewhat idolized him and his quest. He was young and thought that gunfights and tracking outlaws was high adventure, not caustic and deadly.

"Hello, Sandy. How are things going?" Jim replied. "This here is Preacher. Preacher, this is the crew of the Lazy H. I'd say something about them being the lazy part of the brand but they are some of the hardest working hands I've ever seen. Just don't tell them that I ever said such a thing."

The punchers shook hands all around introducing themselves. After the brief introductions, the men all washed up and got ready for their evening repast. They did not want to be late for one of Dinah's meals. Most ranches served the basics, but on the Lazy H good pay and better food kept the hands working hard. Most had never eaten better in their lives.

As they headed for the house, Jim pulled Curly aside. There were plenty of fences that needed mending, so he might as well start now with the one most recently damaged.

"Yeah, boss," Curly said. He wasn't quite sure what he may have done wrong or what was going on. His last conversation with Jim had been somewhat confrontational. For all he knew Jim might be telling him to draw his pay.

"Look, Curly, when I rode out last time, there were some things said that never should have been said."

"I was outta line. You're the boss, not me," the bald puncher interrupted.

"Um, Curly, that's not at all what I meant. What I was going to say is I was way out of line, not you. Even if I am the boss, or one of the bosses, that doesn't give me reason to talk to you or any man the way I did to you."

"What are you saying, boss?"

"What I am saying is, I was the one out of line. You asked a legitimate question and I bit your head off. I'm a bit rusty at this, but I'm trying to apologize. I left you and the whole ranch crew in a lurch and then jumped down your throat for watching out for the ranch's best interest. I acted the fool in more ways than one and I hope you can forgive me."

"Well, uh, don't worry none about that. You back for a while now?"

"I hope so. Thanks, Curly. Now I've got others to talk to, like the rest of the crew, and Tom and Dinah especially. I've been nine kinds of a fool."

"I reckon we've all done that from time to time, boss."

"One other thing, Curly, you can't call me boss anymore." Curly turned quickly and his mouth dropped open. He was stunned.

"I'm Jim. Call me Jim."He stuck out his hand. Curly hesitated a split second. Then realization set in and he took the proffered hand in a strong grip.

Preacher had watched the interaction and smiled. And so it begins. Amends would be made, at least if Curly was any indicator.

Preacher proved to be correct in his assumption. He knew that most people would forgive and let bygones be bygones if you were just willing to ask and admit you were wrong.

Tom took Jim's hand in a powerful grip. "I'm glad you got off that trail. I don't know if you realized it, but you were becoming a killer. Not a fighter or even a man hunter but a killer. Your heart was growing cold. What are your plans now that you are back?"

"I figure to do what I should have been doing all along, work. If you have time later, I would like to talk to you about what we can do to improve the ranch. You know it better than I do."

Jim noticed Dinah looking at Tom like a starving kitten looking at a bowl of cream. "Um, tomorrow of course," he said. "No need to stay up late tonight talking about cows."

After dinner the men trooped out of the house to give Tom time with his family. Jim walked to the graves of his family and stood next to the dogwood that stood like a gnarled sentinel at the head of the graves. He stood silently for a few minutes before speaking. "Ma, Pa, Rachael, I gave them to God. I sent most of them to meet him myself, but I met a friend who taught me something about revenge and justice and grace. I left the last two for God to deal with. He can do it better than I could. I came back to make this place a home like you wanted. Maybe not for me but maybe for Tom and Dinah. They love this place as much as you did. Rest easy." The wind stirred the leaves of the dogwood as if in answer to his words. His family could rest easy. The prodigal was home. He had finally stopped chasing ghosts.

~About the Author~

The son of a WWII era veteran and father of a soldier, Phillip is a decorated military veteran and former drill sergeant himself. Phillip served his country with honor for thirteen years. His love of westerns started at a young age reading such greats as Louis L'Amour and Zane Grey.

He is the author of *Lone Oak* and *Vengeance Is Mine*, with several others in various stages of production. Phillip is dedicated to making his stories the best available in their genre.

www.authorphilhardy.com

9 781946 006820